*Writing as Willa Marsh*

Amy Wingate's Journal
Facing the Music

*Writing as Marcia Willett*

Those Who Serve
Thea's Parrott
The Courtyard
The Dipper
Hattie's Mill
Starting Over
Second Time Around

JOINT L

CW00552304

WITHDRAWN
UPPER NORM

W
Plea
fine
or
ar

L

# Sisters
# Under
# The Skin

## Willa Marsh

UPPER NORWOOD
S.E.19.
ITJ
PUBLIC LIBRARY

SCEPTRE

UPPER NORWOOD
Acc.      C 245
BNB
Cl.        F
Cat'd    24. 2. 98
Code     16.99
PUBLIC LIBRARY

Copyright © Willa Marsh 1998

First published in 1998 by Hodder and Stoughton
A division of Hodder Headline PLC
A Sceptre book

The right of Willa Marsh to be identified as the Author of
the Work has been asserted by her in accordance with the
Copyright, Designs and Patents Act 1988.

10 9 8 7 6 5 4 3 2 1

All rights reserved. No part of this publication may be
reproduced, stored in a retrieval system, or transmitted
in any form or by any means without the prior written
permission of the publisher, nor be otherwise circulated
in any form of binding or cover other than that in which
it is published and without a similar condition being
imposed on the subsequent purchaser.

All characters in this publication are fictitious and any
resemblance to real persons, living or dead, is purely coincidental.

British Library Cataloguing in Publication Data

A CIP catalogue record for this book is
available from the British Library

ISBN 0 340 70797 6


Typeset by Palimpsest Book Production Limited,
Polmont, Stirlingshire
Printed and bound in Great Britain by
Mackays of Chatham PLC, Chatham, Kent

Hodder and Stoughton
A division of Hodder Headline PLC
338 Euston Road
London NW1 3BH

To Nancy and Peter

*∫*

A new summerhouse stands over the dark empty spaces of the old well. The pump has long since disappeared and the slimy rotting boards, which covered the yawning hole, were broken up and thrown down into the black depths before the concrete base was laid and the summerhouse erected. The well was sunk in a small paved tree-shaded yard and, as children, Olivia and Emily were never allowed near this quiet sheltered corner. It is, however, the perfect place for a summerhouse.

'The road will be hidden,' points out Emmy, 'and we shall look across to the hills. If we site the summerhouse carefully we shan't see the road at all.'

'We shall still be able to hear it though,' argues Liv. 'And don't go on about it sounding like the sea. It's a motorway. I *know* it's a motorway. It doesn't sound a bit like the sea.'

When the private detective arrives to make enquiries about Alice, the sisters keep their eyes carefully turned away from the newly-creosoted wooden walls and the comfortable basket chairs set out on the verandah. Instead, they take him into the big kitchen. Whilst they make coffee and find biscuits, Livy and Em discourse quietly together, and with a gentle regret, on the vagaries of their niece: the detective makes unobtrusive notes and throws in an odd question or two. Emmy and Liv murmur about Alice's proclivity for taking off, usually without warning, to foreign fields; her back-packing trips with undesirable companions and the risks involved with hitchhiking. The word 'drugs' is whispered with a kind of anxious horror. They confirm that they have had no letter or telephone call from Alice and ask each other – rather fruitlessly – how long it has been since they saw her. They agree that she has never had much time for her family and speak of the distress and unhappiness she has brought her parents, at which point Emmy becomes visibly emotional and Liv hastens to comfort her.

The detective finishes his coffee, promises to pass on any news he receives and climbs into his car; the two women wave him off, watching until the car reaches the bottom of the drive and passes out through the gateway. They stand together for a moment in silence. The dull roar of the traffic on the motorway is heard more clearly on such a breathlessly hot summer's morning and the smell of creosote mingles with the scent of the honeysuckle which grows over the garage roof. Without speaking they turn their steps towards the summerhouse and seat themselves on the verandah, looking beyond the sloping lawn and the topmost branches of the trees that grow below in the valley; away to the distant hills.

'Try to remember,' says Em, when the question of selling the house arises, 'that this is my home. We have inherited it through *my* mother.'

'But *my* father,' snaps Liv, 'paid the mortgages and the debts. There wouldn't *be* a house without the money he poured into it.'

'Not *quite* the point . . .'

'*Exactly* the point . . .'

'Girls, girls,' cries Rosie, laughing, hands pressed girlishly over her ears. 'Not again. Anyway, *my* mother, *my* father, remember.'

The other two fall silent, drawn together by their mutual antagonism towards Rosie. Rosie: the youngest; the trouble-maker; the Little Princess; child of Mo and Fa.

Thus has it been for fifty years.

Em's father was a fighter pilot, shot down over the Channel. He had been self-confident, boisterous and fond of strong liquor. Orphaned young and raised by a strict, humourless guardian whose ideas were rigidly Victorian, the outbreak of war had been a means of escape and this new freedom was like heady and delicious wine to the young man. He met Maureen at a dance on the RAF station and basked in her uncritical adulation, finding it easy to believe that he was in love with her. Everything was so new and exciting; life was there to be seized with both hands.

Liv's mother was a rising young actress, killed in a direct hit on a London hospital whilst she was entertaining the wounded. She had been self-assertive, devastatingly honest and liked a good time. Her mother and younger sister were living in the south of France when war was declared but she refused to go with them to the safety of America. Fresh from RADA, full of ideals, she intended to use her talents to help the war effort. Edwin's chivalrous and reliable adoration was flattering and something to be relied upon. Both she and the fighter pilot were determined young people, intent on having their own way; amusing, charming and tremendous fun. Attracted at first by these characteristics, their two gentle, sweet-natured partners soon realised their mistake in believing that what they felt for these two larger-than-life people was love; soon – but not soon enough. War fever consumed their common sense and, within weeks of meeting, both couples were married. In July 1940, Olivia was born in Yorkshire and Emily was born in Kent. Three years later the war had deprived each of these children of a parent.

\*     \*     \*

The widow and widower meet at a New Year's party in 1947. They are drawn together by the physical resemblance to the other's late partner. Edwin is stocky and fair, just like the dead fighter pilot; Maureen is slender and dark, very like the dead actress. Here the resemblance ceases – but it is enough to bring them together in the noisy happy crowd; to start them talking to each other. As the party wears on, Edwin and Maureen begin tentatively to exchange histories. After her husband's death, Maureen, with the small Emily, returned to her parents' home. Edwin was lucky enough to resume his career in the bank and has recently been promoted to the dizzy heights of assistant manager.

'My wife would have been so proud,' he tells Maureen mendaciously, knowing full well that the actress considered his career in the bank to be pedestrian and boring and had been mortified whenever he referred publicly to his desk job at Catterick during those early years of the war. She'd discovered that sensitive adoration soon palled into tiresome possessiveness and, as soon as she could, she left Livy with Edwin and his mother and hurried back to London and the stage. 'So proud,' he repeats now, shaking his head a little and smiling bravely but with a touch of pathos.

'I'm sure she would,' murmurs Maureen sympathetically. 'Never mind. You must think of your little girl. Olivia. Such a pretty name.'

'So is Emily. A favourite name of mine,' says Edwin at once, not to be outdone in such courtesies and remembering that the actress had rejected the name as old-fashioned. 'She's a baby not an old aunt,' she'd scoffed. 'We'll call her Olivia; Livy for short.' He'd given in at once.

'Emily is my aunt's name,' muses Maureen reverently, as if this confers some special magic upon it, and, for a fleeting second, Edwin is certain that he hears the actress's husky jeering laugh behind him in the smoky crowded room. 'Emily May. We call her Em, sometimes. You know? E for Emily, M for May.' She laughs lightly at such wantonness but quickly raises her eyebrows, worried at his serious expression. 'Not my aunt,' she hastens to assure him, shocked that he might think she should take such liberties with an elderly lady. 'No, no. My little girl. But we usually call her Emily. I don't really approve of shortening names,' she adds untruthfully, anxious to set his mind quite at rest.

Edwin's expression, however, has nothing to do with Maureen's revelations. He is wondering how he might bind this sensitive, sweet woman to him forever. He sees, with the sudden clarity of vision that just the right amount of alcohol bestows, that this gentle soul is exactly the person he needs to help him deal with Olivia now that his mother has gone to her Great Reward.

'I was just thinking,' he says impulsively, 'that it might be fun for the four of us to get together. You and me and the girls. Tea at Dellers, perhaps? What do you say?'

Repressing the truthful answer, which is 'I thought you'd never ask!' Maureen gives a little cry of delighted surprise. 'What a lovely idea. Perhaps the zoo first . . . ?'

Outside the monkey house Olivia and Emily stare at each other. Since they each resemble their respective mothers they look rather alike; dark hair, brown eyes. Emily has long plaits and wears a kilt and a Fair Isle jersey; Olivia's hair is cut in a pudding basin bob and she wears shorts. The shorts, actually a divided floppy skirt, have been her condition for agreeing to grace this outing with her presence. She hates anything sissy and girlish and, seeing that her father is set on this meeting, she is quick to press her advantage.

'You look so pretty in your Sunday dress,' Edwin pleads. 'And it's January. You'll freeze.'

Olivia watches him with the actress's eyes. 'I never feel cold,' she says.

'You can't wear shorts in January,' says Edwin crossly.

'Then I shan't go,' says Olivia implacably.

Edwin looks approvingly at Emily's delightful kilt and cosy jersey, hoping that Olivia's shorts might be mistaken for a skirt. He has refused to scour the shops for boys' shorts, telling her that she must wait until the summer, and Olivia, who is a skilled bargainer, has settled for this lesser victory. She assesses the anxiously friendly smile on Maureen's face, stares for a moment at Emily's stony expression and turns her back on the whole party. Maureen and Edwin exchange a rueful glance. So it begins.

When the girls realise that Edwin and Maureen intend to marry, despite their individual determination to wreck the relationship, they resign themselves to a sullen obdurate non-co-operation which reduces Maureen to tears and Edwin to frustrated fury. Edwin longs for the conventionality of family life; he sees himself arriving home from a day at the bank to find a sympathetic wife waiting, dinner simmering and his daughter – and his step-daughter – bathed and ready for the bedtime story. Maureen, tired of living with her parents, yearns for Edwin's comfortable town house – not to mention his comfortable salary – and for his gentle, caring protection. Her father revels in the inexorable tyranny of the semi-invalid and her mother's waspish tongue grows more acid as the years pass. Maureen longs to be mistress in her own establishment and, for the first time in seven years, seriously loses her temper with her daughter.

Emily sits on her bed and watches and listens, unmoved, as her mother tells her what a selfish child she is. Presently Maureen changes tack and begins to dwell on the joys of living in a market town. Maureen's parents live on a hill in a large Victorian house, with a village at its gates. Emily has her own room, plenty of space to ride her bicycle and is adept at wheedling things out of her grandmother, nevertheless the future which Maureen is now recklessly painting in vivid colours has certain advantages. Life in the country can be dull and the cinema on Saturday mornings, not to mention dancing lessons and regular teas at Dellers, hold a certain charm.

As Maureen pauses to draw breath, Emily slowly nods her head. 'It might be nice,' she says thoughtfully. Maureen falls on her knees beside her and promises her the dolly she has coveted since their last shopping spree if only she will be reasonable. Emily purses her lips, extends one leg and studies her sandal. Maureen adds the pram and a whole set of clothes for the dolly and Emily smiles, a tiny, sad little smile. 'I'll try,' she says bravely. Maureen embraces her, weak with relief. 'Darling Emmy,' she says, 'I promise you'll never regret it.'

Olivia holds out longer. She is defending her territory.

'I don't want a sister,' she tells Edwin when he begs her to be generous; to welcome Maureen and Emily into her home. 'And I don't want a mummy. Mummies are boring.'

'If we had a mummy,' says Edwin, driven to a low desperate cunning, 'I would buy a car and we could have outings to the seaside and holidays in the country.'

Olivia eats her Marmite soldiers thoughtfully. She longs to do the adventurous exciting things that can only be achieved in the countryside and on the beach. Very few of her friends can boast a motorcar and, living in the town only a few minutes walk from school and the bank, Edwin has so far rejected the idea of a car as an unnecessary expense.

She licks her fingers and looks at him across the table. 'What car?' she asks casually.

Edwin straightens hopefully. 'Well,' he temporises, 'I hadn't got that far. I'd have to look into it.'

Olivia stares at him. 'When we've got the car,' she says, 'we can think about mummies and sisters.'

'Oh, Livy,' he says pleadingly, 'it could be such fun.'

She selects one of the buns which Maureen has made and bites into it. With rationing still in force, and a father who can't cook to save his life, such treats have been rare before Maureen came upon the scene. Olivia considers these aspects of life whilst Edwin watches her anxiously.

'OK,' she says, certain that he will not reprove her for using slang. 'But no car, no mummy. And certainly no sisters.'

Edwin rises and comes round the table to her. 'Darling Livy,' he says, dropping a kiss upon her short dark hair. 'How like your dear mother you are.'

They are married at the end of July, just after the girls have turned eight.

'But I'm not calling him "daddy",' says Emily. 'He's not my daddy. My daddy was a hero.'

Olivia watches this battle from the sidelines with interest. Edwin and Maureen offer Emily a selection; Pa, Pops, Father.

'She can't call me Edwin,' says he. 'It's not . . . not respectful.'

'Oh, I do agree,' agrees Maureen anxiously, 'but we must try not to antagonise her while things are going so well. She's been so good. Perhaps we could think of a jolly little name.'

'Like Mo,' says Olivia, who has been hiding behind the sofa. 'That's what your friends call you, don't they?'

'Well some of them do, dear.' Maureen hides her surprise

– and annoyance – at Olivia's sudden appearance. She decides that this is not quite the moment for a little homily on eavesdropping. 'Those who are my friends and who are special to me. It's a great privilege to use a person's nickname. Rather like your dear papa calling you Livy. You wouldn't want everyone to do that, would you?'

'*You* can call me Livy,' says the child with a devastating smile.

'Well!' Maureen turns pink with gratification and casts a tiny triumphant glance at Edwin. 'Thank you, dear. Thank you, Livy. I feel very privileged.'

'And I,' says Olivia, 'shall call you Mo.'

'You can't,' says Emily, appearing suddenly from behind the long curtains. 'She can't, can she, Mummy?'

'Now, now,' cries Maureen with a little musical laugh, glad that she has not reproved Olivia for eavesdropping. 'No squabbling.'

'If she can call you Mo, then so can I.' Emily glares at Olivia who makes a face at her.

'And why not?' asks Maureen bravely. 'Mo might be short for mother, too, mightn't it?'

'And Fa is short for father,' shouts Emily. 'Mo and Fa. Fa and Mo. Livy and Em. Emmy and Liv. Fa and Mo.'

The girls roll on the floor in ecstasy at the silly names. They pinch and pummel each other, shrieking the names over and over.

'Well,' says Maureen, looking anxiously at Edwin. 'Well . . .'

Edwin gives in. 'Why not?' he asks as he holds out his arms to Maureen. 'If it makes everyone happy.'

Livy and Em rise up to watch them kiss. Livy digs Em in the ribs and Em sniggers. She kicks Livy's ankle.

'What about a ride in the car?' she says thoughtfully.

'Yeah!' breathes Livy. 'Let's go to the beach.'

Edwin releases Maureen and looks doubtfully at his watch.

'Pleeeze,' cry the girls in unison. 'Pleeeze Fa. Pleeeze Mo.'

'Oh, darling,' says Maureen, laughing and flushed at the sudden truce and the friendliness displayed by their two offspring. 'Well, why not? Saturday tomorrow. No school. Let's be devils.'

The girls run off to collect buckets and spades and Maureen and Edwin look at each other with relief.

'It's going to be all right,' they tell each other. 'It was just a matter of time,' and, thus deluded, prepare for a drive to the coast.

So the pattern is set. The girls become skilled political agitators; keeping the relationship on edge; playing off one parent against the other. At first Mo and Fa are so determined not to favour their own child that they go rather too far in the opposite direction when it comes to taking sides or meting out punishments. The girls feel this disloyalty keenly and tears and tantrums ensue.

'You love her better than me,' weeps Emmy to Mo.

'You never made me go to my room before *she* came,' shouts Livy to Fa.

Mo and Fa talk it over and agree that they have been too extreme and that the girls should be reassured. This reassurance finally takes the form of a party dress for Emmy and a kitten for Livy. Peace reigns for a while.

Surprisingly, the question of schooling is easily settled. Emmy is very ready to leave the village school and to go with Livy to the little private school in the town where she wears a smart new green uniform. Livy enjoys the novelty of taking a step-sister to school, having responsibility for her, and Emmy is glad of Livy's confident presence. Because school is neutral ground the girls are able to relax a little and their skills and talents are so divergent that there are no contests. Liv is good at maths and sports; Em loves English and art. With a kind of grudging indifference they offer each other assistance;

'Want any help with your sums?'

'I'll hear your spelling if you like.'

Mo and Fa are delighted, but are – for once – intelligent enough to keep their pleasure hidden. They are careful never to let any feeling of competition disturb this academic truce, but, as Christmas approaches, Mo feels brave enough to re-open the subject of Em's surname. So far she has refused to budge. She is Emily May Grant; Grant was her father's name and it is hers.

'It would be so nice,' pleads Mo, 'if we were all four the same. Wouldn't it, Emmy? Don't you think so? It's so muddly, three Faringdons and one Grant. I know it's a lot to ask . . .'

'She's the odd one out,' observes Liv, who is tired of explaining to people why – if they are sisters – she and Em have different surnames. She has been highly praised at school for the generous way she has taken Em under her wing. Indirectly, her step-sister has brought Liv admiration and attention and she is prepared to allow Em official status as a Faringdon.

'Perhaps,' says Fa, the peacemaker, 'perhaps she might like to add her own name to ours.'

'Grant-Faringdon.' Mo tries it out. 'Oh dear. Sounds a bit pretentious. Faringdon-Grant.' She shakes her head. 'I don't think so.'

Em stares at the tablecloth, enjoying the sensation of being the focus of attention. She senses that changing her name might be the big one: even Livy desires it. Em snuffs up the emanations of Mo's guilt as if it is blood in her nostrils and prepares for the kill.

'It's not fair to Daddy,' she says, gently but reproachfully. 'We might forget him altogether if I don't have his name any more.'

For Mo and Fa it is as if, for one terrible moment, the fighter pilot is present at the breakfast table. Fa is conscious of a strong feeling of shame. He, for one, has been only too ready to sink the memory of the fighter pilot. Mo's guilt increases and she wonders how much Em has suffered at the loss of her father and whether she has been selfish in seeking happiness at Em's expense.

'Oh, darling,' she says quickly. 'Of course we shall never forget him.'

Em stares at her accusingly. 'You've forgotten him already. You never talk about him any more.'

Liv, who knows a good thing when she sees it, enters the fray. 'Fa doesn't talk about Mummy any more, either,' she tells Em sadly.

It is as if a message passes between them.

'Daddy was a hero,' Em tells her wistfully. 'Mummy – Mo, I mean – used to be so proud of him. She was always telling me about him. He shot down hundreds of Germans.'

('Perhaps not quite hundreds, darling,' mutters Mo edgily.)

'My Mummy was an actress,' confides Livy to Em. 'She was very beautiful. Daddy – Fa, I mean – used to wait for her at the stage door night after night and take her flowers. Everyone adored her.'

('Perhaps not quite everybody, Liv,' mutters Fa testily.)

'I've got a photograph of Daddy in uniform,' begins Em – but Mo has had enough.

'Goodness me! Look at the time,' she says brightly. 'Aren't we going Christmas shopping?'

Are they? The girls eye her speculatively. Has she taken the bait? She is nodding meaningfully to Fa across the table and he is getting up in a relieved and breezy kind of way.

'We certainly are. Toyshop first, I think.' He gives Liv a little pat and winks at Emmy. 'I hope you've both made your lists for Father Christmas.'

Emmy and Liv look at each other across the tablecloth and exchange a smile.

'I'm terribly worried about Em,' says Mo to Fa later.

'You sound like Mrs Dale,' says Fa, who has spent rather more than he can afford on Christmas presents.

'I wonder if I was as understanding as I might have been when her father was killed.'

'I'm sure you were,' says Fa, who has had quite enough of the fighter pilot for one day. 'She was far too young to be really affected by it.'

'She was barely three,' says Mo unhappily. 'She was at a difficult age.'

'Who isn't?' mutters Fa.

Just when things are beginning to settle down a little, Mo becomes pregnant. She is so happy that she longs to tell everybody, especially Livy and Em. Fa is wiser. He counsels her to wait; nine months is a long time for small girls to contain their impatience for a dear little brother or sister. Mo sees the wisdom of this and manages to control her excitement although she begins to knit and sew tiny garments while the girls are at school. She returns regularly to her parents' large house on the hill and roots about in the spacious attic, unearthing Emmy's crib and the large Silver Cross pram which she brings down to be cleaned. She hums to herself as she fetches cloths and polish and opens the hood to check for deterioration.

Her mother watches the proceedings with a sardonic eye. She has no illusions about how the girls will react when they know about the baby and she is over-protective about Emmy, jealous for her rights.

'How will she feel about it having her pram?' she asks, watching Mo rubbing busily at the coachwork.

'Please Mother,' says Mo with a patient brightness. 'We've

been through this before. And don't call the baby "it". After all, this was my pram before it was Emmy's. We kept it just in case she had a little brother or sister. Just as well, isn't it?'

She laughs gaily, hoping to jolly the old dear up a bit; she has been rather odd since Mo's father died. Her mother continues to regard her with menopausal gloom.

'But it's not her brother or sister, is it?' she asks.

'Of course it is,' snaps Mo, her patience beginning to fray a little. 'He or she will be her step-brother or step-sister. This baby is a very special one. He or she will link us together as a proper family.'

'Honestly,' says her mother, glancing at her watch and wondering if it's rather too early for her pre-lunch gin, 'I wonder about you sometimes.'

'I know you don't care for Fa,' Mo begins, her voice low with unexpected anger, 'and I know you feel that Livy has put Em's nose out of joint but is it too much to ask that you try to be happy for me?'

'Why do you need *me* to be happy for you?' asks her mother, who does indeed find Fa dull and Livy pushy. She cherished a secret passion for the fighter pilot (who kissed her once when they'd both had several drinks too many) and wonders how Maureen can settle for the quiet, gentle Edwin. '*You're* happy. *He's* happy. What more do you want?'

'Nothing!' cries Mo, flinging the duster on the hall floor. Her back aches and she feels weepy. 'Nothing. Forget it. I don't want anything.'

'You need a drink,' says her mother, feeling brighter now that she has made Mo lose her temper. 'Just a nip. Come on.'

'Where do you get your supply from?' asks Mo, when she gets a glimpse of the bottles stored in the cupboard.

'Mind your own business,' says her mother, pouring. 'Bloody rationing.'

'I hope it won't hurt the baby,' says Mo anxiously.

'Do it good to have some gin in its veins rather than skim and water.' Mo's mother gulps back her tot and feels the suicidal tendencies that so often threaten to overwhelm her receding a little. She regards her daughter maliciously. 'Told the girls yet?'

'No.' Mo is enjoying the warm gin-induced feeling which relaxes her. 'Not yet. It's going to be *such* a surprise for them.'

Mo's mother laughs until she chokes. 'You're so right,' she says when she can speak. 'Let's have another.'

'I'm terribly worried about Mother,' Mo tells Fa later that evening.

'Have you ever thought about keeping a diary?' he asks. He knows that Mo's mother dislikes him and he finds it difficult to be as caring as he should be for her welfare. 'What's the matter now?'

'Don't say it like that.' The gin has left Mo feeling irritable. 'She's at that difficult age.'

'Who isn't?' mutters Fa.

The news is let out of the bag by a neighbour whom Mo and the girls meet on the doorstep as they come home from the shops. Mo has been unable to resist telling her the good news although she swears her to secrecy. Unfortunately the neighbour doesn't see the girls, who are just inside the door, and she beams encouragingly at Mo.

'You're looking so well,' she says. 'When's the baby due? You take care now . . .'

Mo shuts the door hastily, but it is too late. Livy and Em are waiting for her, standing shoulder to shoulder.

'What baby?' asks Em. 'What's she talking about?'

Flustered, Mo hurries them through to the kitchen and fills the kettle so as to give herself time to think. She is almost relieved that the truth is out at last. She turns to face them, blushing a little.

'We have some wonderful news,' she tells them. 'I'm expecting a dear little baby. In the spring you'll both have a little baby brother or sister.'

She examines their faces, waiting for joy to break through, and feels the first faint thrill of anxiety.

'We don't want a baby,' says Emmy speaking for both of them.

'Aren't you a bit old,' asks Liv, 'to be having babies?'

'Oh dear.' Mo tries to smile but she feels hurt and oddly frightened. 'No, of course I'm not too old. Now don't tell me you're jealous! Good heavens!' cries Mo, laughing at such a ridiculous notion. 'As if you could be jealous of a poor little baby when we both love you so much . . .' But she is talking to herself. With one accord the girls have whirled out of the kitchen and up the stairs.

'I'm terribly worried about the girls,' says Mo later to Fa.

'Perhaps you should have married a doctor,' says Fa.

'They know about the baby,' says Mo distractedly, 'and they're not at all pleased. Do you think that Mother might be right?'

'Who knows?' asks Fa, meaning 'who cares?' He is tired and is suffering from indigestion. Austerity Britain is getting him down and two girls and a wife are expensive to run; so is the car. Now there's the baby to worry about. 'They'll get used to the idea. You'll just have to be firm with them.'

'We must be sensitive and understanding,' says Mo reproachfully, although she feels faintly resentful at the general lack of support and sympathy for a woman in her condition. *Is* she perhaps too old to be having babies? 'They're at a very difficult age.'

'Who isn't?' mutters Fa.

\*     \*     \*

Emmy and Liv draw closer together. Livy knows all about babies. In earlier happier days she has come upon Fa in his bath and is fascinated by his equipment. She demands facts and explanations from the blushing, dripping Fa who tries to wrap himself in a towel whilst his daughter pokes at his private places. Despite his embarrassment, he tells her about seeds and eggs and love; he also explains how the baby arrives. Livy, at five years old, is bored stiff long before he finishes.

Now she recounts it, with certain embellishments, to the ignorant Emmy. They huddle together on Emmy's bed and try to imagine Mo and Fa doing the things which Livy has just described. Instinctively, they recognise the need to laugh at such bizarre behaviour; laughter pushes away the fear and that insecurity of adulthood which edges nearer whilst Livy is whispering to Em. They retreat gratefully into the known safe world of childhood, glad that they need not understand just yet.

They begin to giggle, hands over mouths, eyes watching sharply, urging the other to greater excesses of mirth. They roll about helplessly and then lie panting, testing to see if they are back to normal, the fear gone . . .

'So here you are!' Mo puts her head round the door. 'I could hear you laughing. How lovely to hear you sounding so happy. It's nearly lunchtime.'

They look at her, sensing her need. Emmy smiles.

'We were thinking,' she says, 'that we might go and see Grandmother this afternoon. Just me and Liv on our own. On the bus.'

So far this treat has been denied them.

'Yes,' says Liv. 'You can have a rest. Put your feet up.'

'That's very thoughtful of you.' Mo feels confused. She longs to accept the olive branch but she and Fa have agreed that the bus journey out into the country and the long walk from the bus stop is rather ambitious for two little girls on their own.

'I can show Livy the pram and the cot,' says Em.

This is the first reference to the existence of the baby that either of them has made.

'Oh, *pleeeze*,' says Liv.

They stand together, shoulder to shoulder, smiling at her and Mo's relief and gratitude is so great that she gives in. They go to her and hug her – but gently so as not to hurt the baby. They kiss her and pat the bump tenderly, grinning at one another privately.

'Oh, darlings,' she says, tears in her eyes. 'Very well. But you must telephone from Grandmother's to say that you've arrived safely. Oh dear, I hope Fa won't be cross.'

'Fa should be here looking after you,' says Livy solicitously, 'instead of playing golf all day.'

Mo laughs. 'Oh poor Fa. He has to have *some* fun. Now come down and have lunch and I'll telephone Grandmother to ask her if she'll meet you from the bus.'

'Been listening to *Mrs Dale's Diary*?' asks Fa cheerfully when he comes in late. He has won a very small cup and has been celebrating.

'No,' says Mo. She sees that there will be no difficulties in explaining about the girls who are back safely and tucked up in bed. His question strikes her as odd and this apparent obsession irritates her. 'What makes you ask?' she says sharply.

'Oh, I don't know,' says Fa. 'Just thought you might have been.'

# 3

Rosamunde is born late on Easter Saturday. Mo remembers to buy Easter eggs for the girls but Fa forgets to give them to Liv and Emmy before he rushes off to the maternity wing of the cottage hospital early on Easter morning. Liv climbs on to the kitchen chair and reaches into the cupboard for the eggs. The girls sit at the kitchen table and eat two each before breakfast, cross that Fa has forgotten them. It is the first black mark against Rosie. They are taken in to see her and stare down at this pale fair creature, lying in a cot beside Mo's bed. Mo looks pale too; pale but happy. Fa is beside himself with pride.

'She has your colouring,' Mo tells him and they smile tenderly at one another.

'Want to hold your little sister?' asks the nurse.

Emmy shakes her head but, aware of the glances of the other patients, Livy perches on Mo's bed, spreads her skirts and holds out her arms prettily. Rosie is placed into them and everyone – except Em – clucks and smiles approvingly.

Back home, without the audience, things are different. Livy soon tires of being Mummy's Little Helper and Emmy is so jealous she can hardly speak. For the first time, Mo and Fa are indifferent to sulks and tempers. To begin with, Mo tries to draw the girls into the charmed circle but she finds

that there is less time now for coaxing and wheedling. Fa
is detailed to take them out, read the bedtime stories, help
them with their schoolwork, but he, too, wearies of their
unresponsive coolness and grumpy faces.

Rosie is such a pretty, happy baby. As the summer draws
on Mo and Fa are generally to be found hanging over the
pram or cot, talking in silly voices and congratulating each
other on their cleverness in producing the perfect child.
They still go to the beach, but now Emmy and Liv are told
to be careful not to joggle the carrycot in the car; they are
warned against kicking up sand on the beach, lest Rosie
gets it in her eyes. Mo fusses about the position of the
sunshade and Fa won't swim with the girls because Mo
has fallen asleep and someone has to be at hand to watch
over the baby.

In desperation Livy and Em decide to join the enemy.
They begin to take a spurious interest in Rosie, hoping to
win attention and praise, but Livy is careless and Emmy is
clumsy and Mo is not quite so patient as she has been in
the past. Her mother is ill and the town house is beginning
to feel crowded. Exhausted by the daily trips to see her
mother, Mo suggests that they all move back to the house
on the hill.

Fa thinks it through carefully. Would living in a big house
in the country be compensation enough for putting up with
Mo's mother? Since Mo's father died the house and garden
have fallen into a certain amount of disrepair but a recent
legacy from an uncle, along with the money from the town
house, should go a long way towards putting things right.
He sees the advantage of having a garden big enough for
the girls to get lost in and rather fancies himself as a country
gentleman.

'It would be lovely,' says Mo wistfully, 'for Rosie to be
brought up in the country in peacetime. Livy and Em have
missed so much.'

to

*     *     *

They move just after the girls' tenth birthdays. They are
given bicycles since they now have room to ride them and
for a while all is new and exciting. Emmy shows Liv the
best trees to climb in the orchard and the safest place to
paddle in the little stream. The house is big and cool and
seems enormous after the comfortable cosiness of the town
house. In the winter it will be draughty and difficult to heat
but now the doors and windows are left wide open to let in
the sun and the spacious rooms, with their high ceilings, are
full of light.

Mo fills every jug and vase with roses from the garden.
She hurries to and fro, her feet tapping from wooden floor
to thick rugs, happy to be home again. Fa decorates the
nursery and wonders if they might afford to re-modernise
the kitchen. Grandmother is confined to her big south-
facing bedroom and Mo is able to imagine that the house is
truly hers. Livy and Em often creep in to see Grandmother.
Sometimes she is heavily asleep; at others she is lucid and
encourages them to sit beside her. Old Janet, who has
helped in the house since she was a girl, fills Grandmother's
silver flask with colourless liquid which she sips from time
to time. The girls assume that it is water.

'It smells funny,' says Em, sniffing at it as she screws the
top back on the flask.

'So it does.' Grandmother chuckles to herself. 'Never
mind. Don't tell Mummy.'

The girls would never betray Grandmother, who has been
an ally ever since that first visit on the bus, but one night
the top is not screwed on properly and the flask is knocked
over. Mo, coming in to say goodnight, discovers her mother
awash with gin. Old Janet is dismissed and Grandmother
begins to be possessed of sudden rages which mean that she
has to be given things to make her sleep for longer periods.
She becomes sullen and withdrawn, the girls visit her less

and, when the school holidays arrive, spend most of their days outside.

They are forbidden to go into the courtyard which houses the unused well. Fa removes the pump and puts a heavy wooden cover over the hole. The girls play hide and seek amongst the rhododendron bushes and eat raspberries in the high-walled kitchen garden. They make themselves a house in a deserted shed with old pieces of furniture found in the attics and build a dam in the stream. For hours together they are able to forget that they have a baby sister – until Rosie begins teething. She screams well into each night and is fretful and sick. Fa and Mo are distressed by her suffering and become tired through lack of rest.

Tempers grow short. The girls are continually being told to make less noise, to be more helpful and are given holiday tasks. Livy is severely reprimanded for dropping her bicycle noisily on the terrace and waking Rosie, who has just dropped off to sleep after a prolonged screaming spell. Emmy has her legs slapped for cheeking Mo and accidentally-on-purpose smashing a bottle of milk. Their sulks impress neither Mo nor Fa and they are denied new scooters which are all the rage. Fa gives them a lecture on economics and Grandmother puts the lid on things by dying suddenly in the night. Only Rosie continues to receive unconditional love and undivided attention.

'I hate her,' mutters Em.

'I wish *she'd* die in the night,' thinks Livy.

On the morning of Grandmother's funeral, the girls are left at home. Mo thinks they are too young to attend the service and arranges for old Janet's successor, who helps out twice a week, to come up to keep an eye on the children and prepare the funeral lunch. It is early September; high cumuli hide the sun but it is a bright warm day. A pheasant churrs in the meadow below the garden and a hawk hangs motionless above the sharp golden stubble of a newly-cut field. The church bell has stopped ringing; a dog barks and falls silent.

Betty is busy in the kitchen, helped by a self-important Livy, but Emmy has slipped away and is on the terrace. The pram stands as usual outside the long windows of the breakfast room; there are no cries, no sign of waving fists. With the toe of her sandal, Em pokes at the moss growing between the flagstones, her eye on the pram. Mo has been so distracted by grief and the organisation of the funeral that she has forgotten to fix the cat-net in place. Em advances a step or two. Between her fingers, hidden in her pocket, she rolls a berry plucked from the deadly nightshade that grows in the wood which edges the garden beyond the stream.

She remembers her nature classes and Miss Taylor pointing out the plants which must never be touched; berries which must never be eaten.

'The black berry of the deadly nightshade is *extremely* poisonous. Bittersweet is often miscalled deadly nightshade . . .'

Em sees the pictures in her head as she watches the pram. Silently she approaches and stares down. It gives her a shock to see that Rosie's eyes are wide open; her cheeks are patchy red and there is dribble bubbling out of her mouth. One tooth is through but there are more to come. Rosie smiles gummily to her sister and reaches out to her. Carefully, slowly, eyes and ears alert, Emmy brings out the berry, unwraps it from her grubby handkerchief and carefully introduces it into Rosie's mouth. She gurgles frothily whilst Emmy watches, breath suspended, heart crashing in her chest. To her horror the berry immediately re-appears at the corner of the dribbling mouth and slides down the wet chin. Rosie crams a fist against her gums and begins to wail loudly. Footsteps can be heard approaching. With a quick glance towards the house, Emmy snatches up the berry and beats a quick retreat.

\*     \*     \*

Livy, sent by Betty to check on Rosie, sees the flick of Em's
skirt and guesses that she has been teasing the baby. She
crosses the terrace and looks at Rosie, leaning into the pram
to put the teething ring into her hand. Rosie begins to gnaw
on it and her cries fade away. Livy suddenly notices that
the cat-net is not in place, braces herself to run back to
the kitchen to report it . . . and hesitates. Stretched out
on the gravel, Boswell, Livy's large tortoiseshell cat is fast
asleep. Livy broods thoughtfully. Rosie gurgles quietly. The
sun has dispelled the thin cloud and Livy feels it hot on her
shoulders, burning through her yellow Aertex shirt.

She glances around and, treading quickly and lightly, she
speeds across the terrace and picks Boswell up in her arms.
He is not pleased at being disturbed but suffers himself to be
hauled back to the pram. With another careful look about
her, Livy leans over and deposits him on Rosie's face. Her
gurglings are stifled but Boswell is not so comfortable as he
was on the drive. Rosie struggles beneath his weight and
the teething ring sticks in his groin. With a hiss and a growl
he resists Livy's restraining hands and leaps from the pram,
scratching Rosie's face in the process.

Her shrieks this time are deafening. She is frightened and
hurt and Livy feels weak with terror as Betty comes out
at a run.

'Oh, Betty,' screams Livy, with astonishing presence of
mind. 'Come quick. Boswell was in the pram. Mo forgot to
put the cat-net on. I frightened him away but he's scratched
Rosie. She's bleeding.'

Her guilt and fear enable her to put up a splendid performance and, by the time the funeral party return, the place
is in an uproar and the doctor has been summoned. Emmy,
who has watched the entire performance, is impressed.
She wonders whether she should tell Livy what she has
seen but decides to keep her knowledge to herself for the

time being. She feels it might come in useful one day. Livy, however, has become a Little Heroine; she has saved Rosie's life. She, too, has received a few scratches from Boswell's scrabbling claws and her hands are bathed and she is promised a reward for such bravery. Em is unable to remain silent.

'I saw you,' she whispers, when they are getting ready for bed. 'I saw what you did.'

'And I saw *you*,' says Liv at once, remembering the flick of Em's skirt and Rosie's wails. 'I know what you'd been doing.'

Liv only guesses that Em was teasing Rosie but guilt makes Emmy flush and her hand goes to her pocket. 'She spat it out,' she says defensively. 'It didn't hurt her.'

'What was it?' asks Liv curiously.

Emmy takes out her handkerchief and together they look at the berry, squashed now and withering. Liv, too, remembers Miss Taylor's warnings.

'Is it . . . deadly nightshade?'

Em nods. Liv is impressed but they are both frightened. They remember how the doctor examined Rosie and the questions he asked. The risks are too great.

'Throw it away,' advises Liv. 'If you won't tell about Boswell, I won't tell about the berry.'

When Livy is asked to choose her reward she says that she will only accept if Em is given something, too. Touched by her generosity and delighted by the bond which has grown between the two girls, Mo and Fa buy them the long-coveted scooters. Livy basks in their love and approval for a few days until suddenly Rosie learns to crawl and Livy finds she is back on the outside with Emmy.

Boswell is put down.

'I just couldn't risk it happening again,' Mo tells Livy with tears in her eyes. 'I'm so sorry, darling, but you must see how I couldn't. When Rosie is bigger we'll have another cat . . .'

Livy weeps in private and blames Rosie. It seems quite simple to her: if Rosie had not been born, Boswell would still be alive.

# 4

When Livy and Em are twelve, Livy's aunt Pamela arrives from America. She is very sleek and expensive and smells delicious and Fa suddenly remembers exactly how he felt about her sister – the actress – when he first met her. He stands up straighter and pays Pamela daring compliments. The cellar is lavishly restocked and Fa is taught, with many shrieks and nudges, how to make a cocktail.

Mo goes about thin-lipped and silent and, when Pamela recounts amusing anecdotes, Mo's faint dismissive smile does not reach her eyes. She is in danger of disliking Fa intensely and begins to notice things about him that she has hitherto missed . . .

Does he know how silly he looks, she wonders, when he raises one eyebrow so affectedly after making a particularly foolish joke? Should she tell him that he is very nearly bald on the crown of his head?

'Does she have to call you "hon"?' she asks Fa, irritably. 'It sounds so German.'

'Not that sort of Hun, darling,' laughs Fa. Why has she never noticed how annoying his laugh is? 'It's short for "honey". It's a term of endearment.'

'I'm well aware of that,' snaps Mo.

Livy and Em are fascinated by this dazzling creature and

Livy is delighted to be the owner of such a glamorous aunt. Pamela tells her how much she resembles her dead mother, the actress, and buys her presents. She is careful, however, not to put Emmy's nose out of joint, but Emmy is too besotted to be looking for slights. They trail about after her like two little dogs and she chats away to them whilst she dresses for dinner, as though they are her contemporaries. She dabs her scent behind their ears and lets them try her lipsticks; she wraps a long silk scarf round Em's throat and fastens a pretty brooch to Liv's jersey. When they try to return them later, she shakes her head. 'Keep 'em, hon. Plenty more where they came from.' Best of all, she does not seem to care for Rosie. She is unaffected by Rosie's latest funny little sayings or how sweet she looks when she's had her bath. Pamela avoids the bath scene; she is downstairs with Fa making cocktails and letting Emmy and Liv have 'sippers' as she calls them.

Mo skulks on the landing, listening to the shrieks, resentful and hurt. Fa has not been upstairs to read to Rosie for ages; not since Pamela arrived. Mo goes downstairs and, head held high, she stalks past the open drawing-room door en route to the kitchen. She bangs about with saucepans and crashes plates. Fa appears. There is a foolish smile hanging on his lips and his hair is ruffled; Mo can smell Pamela's scent on his jacket.

'Anything I can do?' he asks.

'I don't know,' returns Mo cuttingly. '*Is* there anything you can do?'

The words 'except make a fool of yourself with that woman' remain unspoken on the air. Fa hangs about in the doorway, one ear cocked towards the drawing room. He knows that Mo is jealous and he is aware of, and is enjoying, an uncharacteristic sense of power. He is proud that once he was able to make a girl like Pamela's sister love him and he feels that there is no harm in letting Mo see that he has not always been a rather dull, family man. She has turned away from him and is fiddling with the oven and Fa shrugs and returns to the drawing room.

Before she leaves, Pamela raises the subject of the girls' education. She has listened closely to Livy and Em and has come to the conclusion that it might be sensible if they were to be sent away to school for a few years. She offers to pay for Livy and suggests the school where she and her sister were very happy.

Mo is up in arms at once . . .

'I think we know best as to what is right for our daughters,' she says with an acid smile.

'Oh, honey,' says Pamela, shaking her head. 'Can't you see that the last people who should have children are parents?'

Fa giggles and Mo glares at him. 'Do you have children?' she asks Pamela sweetly, knowing perfectly well that she hasn't.

'No, I don't,' admits Pamela, 'but your two girls are dying to go to boarding school and it would give you and Ed more time together. I'm sure the girls would benefit.'

*Ed*! Mo feels that she might burst.

'Perhaps if they were boys we might feel differently. *Edwin* and I,' says Mo, 'like to have our girls about us. Perhaps Americans feel differently . . .'

'Hold on there,' protests Pamela. 'I'm English, too, remember.'

'I'd never have guessed it,' murmurs Mo.

'It's a very generous offer,' says Edwin awkwardly. 'Isn't it Mo? We're very grateful.'

'We have made a rule,' says Mo, restraining her gratitude without any visible effort, 'to treat Livy and Em exactly the same. I think it's most unlikely that we could afford the expense. The war has hit us very hard. Of course, I know that you hardly noticed it in America . . .'

'Mo!' says Fa warningly. He smiles placatingly at her. 'There's the money that your mother left in trust for Emmy. Perhaps we should think about this. It might be wrong to deprive them of such an opportunity.'

Mo sits in silence. She is mortified that Fa should take Pamela's part and that he should discuss their private affairs in front of her. Pamela stands up, sends Fa a tiny complicit wink, and gives a huge yawn.

'I'm for bed,' she says. 'Think it over why don't you?' At the door she pauses. 'And if you decide to go for it, take my advice and send them to different schools.'

'Which just goes to show,' cries the overwrought Mo, 'that she knows nothing – *nothing*! – about children and especially about Emmy and Liv. Not only would they hate to be sent away to school, they certainly wouldn't hear of being separated . . .'

She is wrong. Naughty Pamela tells the girls about the chance that has been offered to them and they are wild with excitement. Have they not read every one of Enid Blyton's school stories? Do they not long for midnight feasts; to play lacrosse? The genes of the actress and the fighter pilot are strong within them. They long to experiment, explore, test themselves. They long to get away from Mo and Fa and – most especially – from Rosie.

They plead to be allowed to go away to school. Reeling from the shock, Mo is chagrined to find that Emmy and Liv are also very ready to be parted from each other. They sense that the time has come to make a change and they are ready for it. For four years they have been Livy and Em; Emmy and Liv. Mo has even arranged it so that they have their birthdays on the same day, exactly half way between the two dates. They even share a cake with twice the amount of candles. Mo dresses them identically, as if they are twins. They long to break free and establish the identity of their own personalities.

'It might be rather fun to have time together,' suggests Fa, hoping that Mo will come to terms with it. He knows that he has made rather a fool of himself over Pamela and is anxious to make amends; to become Fa, the family man again. Or better still; Fa the lover. Pamela has set his hormones tingling and he suddenly sees that it would be fun to be alone with Mo. After all, Rosie is only two years old . . .

Mo is determined not to be too ready to be won round but she is beginning to see some of the advantages. It might be rather nice to have conversations with Fa without being conscious of sharp ears; to share embraces without worrying about prying eyes. Now that Pamela has gone, Mo has stopped disparaging Fa and is seeing him as Pamela saw him. It might be rather fun to be free, to play a little. After all, Rosie is only two years old . . .

Emmy and Liv are surprised at the ease with which they carry the day. Separate schools are chosen for them. Liv's is strongly biased towards the sciences and sport; Emmy's specialises in the arts. Everybody is happy.

Rosie especially is happy. She grows up in a hothouse atmosphere of adoration and generosity. Everything of which the war deprived Livy and Em is heaped upon Rosie a hundredfold. In other words, she is spoiled rotten. She does not have to scheme and bribe – as Livy and Em had – to have her own way. It falls naturally to her lot to have rose leaves strewn in her path. She is blonde and blue-eyed, like Fa, slim and supple, like Mo, but has inherited none of their sweet, gentle genes. She is a cross between Mo's cunning old mother and Fa's selfish old father. It is an awesome combination. On the rare occasions when her wishes are not immediately granted, she does not sulk or glower. She climbs winningly onto Fa's lap and pats his face with her little hands and kisses him, snuggling her soft cheek into his neck. Fa has never had this kind of affection from the small Livy, who was independent and sassy, and he loves it. 'My little Princess,' he murmurs, cuddling Rosie close, and Mo's eyes fill with tears when she sees them so.

By five, Rosie has Mo and Fa weighed off and tied up. By the time she is ten, Iago could have taken her correspondence course and learned a trick or two. When her sisters come home for the holidays, Rosie studies them carefully. It is not too long before she realises the right way to proceed. She has never heard the words 'divide and rule' but this is exactly what she does.

When they meet up in the holidays, Emmy and Liv have much to discuss. There is a certain amount of rivalry, of course; a touch of 'my school is better than your school' – but on the whole they are pleased to see one another. They are not quite so pleased to see Rosie but 'absence makes the heart grow fonder' and they are ashamed when they remember how they tried to kill this pretty little girl. To begin with, they are prepared to put her in her pushchair and wheel her down to the village. The locals are used to Rosie's charms and are more interested in Livy and Em, so the girls are happy enough to pass a few hours thus. They listen tolerantly to Rosie's latest sayings and even read to her at bedtime, but are more than ready to return to school and to their own friends and interests.

By the time Rosie is five and the girls are fifteen, acrimony is creeping into the relationship between Emmy and Liv. It is rather flattering when Rosie curls up on Em's bed and asks, 'Will you read to me tonight, Emmy?'

Emmy studying her face in the looking glass – is that a

spot coming? – says absently, 'Isn't it Liv's turn? She's been looking out one of her old books specially.'

Rosie wriggles, pouting a little, and her voice is wheedling when she says, 'But you read better than she does. I like it when you do all the voices. *Pleeeze*, Emmy.'

Emmy is gratified but she tries to be fair. She looks at Rosie through the glass whilst she says, 'I think you ought to listen to Liv's story tonight. Ask her to do the voices, too.'

Rosie, seeing that she is being watched, makes a pleading face at her sister as she says, 'But I want *you*, Em. *Pleeeze*.'

Pleased to be wanted, to be preferred, Em laughs indulgently and says, 'OK. I don't suppose Liv will really mind.'

Rosie runs out of the room and presently finds Livy sitting in the swing and doing a crossword.

'Let's swing together,' she says, scrambling up on to Livy's lap.

'You're a pest,' says Livy, but she puts down her book and pencil and pushes off.

Rosie clings tightly round her waist, beaming up at her sister, and Liv thinks that perhaps she's not such a bad kid after all.

'I've found the book,' she says. 'It was up in the attic. It's called *The Secret Travellers*. I told you, didn't I? It's about an otter and a squirrel and a badger who set off to find the end of the world. Actually, I'm looking forward to reading it again myself . . . What's wrong?'

'Oh, Liv,' wails Rosie. 'But Emmy said you didn't want to read to me any more. She says you think it's boring. She says she'll read to me tonight.'

'But I've found the book now,' says Liv, hurt. It's true that she has said that the nightly reading sessions are boring but she has been looking forward to sharing this story with her small sister. 'I spent hours looking for it.'

'She says she'll read it,' says Rosie, slyly watching Liv's face. 'She says she's a better reader than you are. You don't do the voices properly, she says. Can't read for toffee.'

Livy is silent for a moment. 'OK then.' Her voice is flat.

She slows the swing, shrugging Rosie from her lap and picks up her book and pencil. When Em comes out a little later and asks Liv if she's ready for a jaunt on the bus to town, Livy doesn't look up.

'No thanks,' she says.

Emmy is puzzled. It has been more or less settled at breakfast that they will go together.

'Come on,' she says. 'It's market day. You said you needed some stockings.'

'Changed my mind,' says Liv, pretending to fill in a word.

'Come *on*,' pleads Em. 'It's not so much fun on my own.'

'I don't feel like it,' shouts Liv. 'Just leave me alone.'

She slips off the swing and goes into the house. Em frowns, shrugs, and sets off down the path alone. Rosie creeps out from behind the rhododendrons and, humming to herself, hoists herself up onto the swing.

# 5

When Livy and Em leave school Fa suggests that they should be enrolled on a secretarial course. He insists that they must be able to support themselves if necessary. Careers for women are not, in general, regarded with any great seriousness in the late fifties and Mo and Fa are not the kind of parents to imagine their daughters as doctors or lawyers. Livy and Em, glad to be free of timetables and routine, groan at the thought of more studying, but Fa is firm for once and they reluctantly submit. They are, however, looking forward to a few weeks of freedom before the course starts in the autumn. They play tennis on the lawn, go to the pictures together and spend hours talking, trying out new hairstyles, exchanging clothes. For once it is fun to look alike; heads turn to look after them and they giggle and flirt knowing that there is safety in numbers. They are inseparable. The telephone begins to ring almost continually; bashful boys; eager boys; confident boys. They all want to see more of Emmy and Liv.

Mo decides to give a big party. The house which faces south west, is a perfect setting; its red brick walls mellowed by age and covered by wisteria and clematis; the high large rooms full of sunshine; the paved terrace looking out over the lawns. The breakfast room is cleared so that the young people can dance after dinner to the gramophone; there will be bridge for their parents in the drawing room. Mo and Fa are so proud of their girls as they show their party frocks; they are so young and fresh and pretty. Em and Livy twirl self-consciously, making faces at each other, happy and excited. Mo and Fa have tears in their eyes; even Rosie is temporarily forgotten.

The girls absolutely refuse to allow Rosie to stay up for dinner on the night of the party.

'She's much too young,' they cry. 'She'll ruin everything.'

They know only too well how she is able to draw attention to herself; even the attention of young men supposedly besotted by her elder sisters. Rosie hangs round Mo as she checks lists and makes out invitations. She does not whine; she just makes her sad presence felt. Mo feels guilty but accepts that this is the girls' big day and that it must be just as they wish. Anyway, Rosie *is* too young for an evening party. In the end, she goes to stay with a school-friend – but her defeat rankles . . .

Rosie watches and listens from behind doors and curtains; a shadow on the landing catching whispered secrets; a soft footfall in the badly lit corridor by the telephone. The party over, the harmony between Livy and Em begins to disintegrate. Secrets are leaked; boyfriends hear – oh, so innocently – that they are mocked in private; Fa discovers – quite by accident – that Livy has overspent on her allowance; Mo finds out – purely by chance – that Emmy has been to the pictures with an undesirable young man who has been forbidden the house. Liv finds her last pair of silk stockings, laddered and quite ruined, in Emmy's room. Em, looking for her favourite nail varnish, finds the empty bottle in Livy's wastepaper basket.

Arguments spring up. Accusations and recriminations ring through the house where there was once laughter and friendship. Emmy throws Liv's newly-whitened tennis shoes in the water butt twenty minutes before a match at the local club: Livy empties a packet of tea over Em's newly-set hair half an hour before she is due to set out for a dance.

                        *        *        *

'I'm terribly worried about the girls,' says a distraught Mo.

'Is *Mrs Dale's Diary still* running?' asks Fa.

'Everything was going so well,' keens Mo. 'That lovely party . . .'

The lovely party has set Fa back a pound or two and he is in financial difficulties. He is tired of the ingratitude and selfishness of children. 'It's time they were out earning some money,' he grumbles. 'They've got too much time on their hands.'

'They're at a difficult age,' excuses Mo.

'Oh Christ!' mutters Fa. 'Not that again.'

Emmy does not do too well with her secretarial studies but she is offered a job as receptionist at the large hotel in the town. She enjoys meeting the guests and the bustle of arrivals and departures; even the inconvenience of unsocial hours is a novelty. She works hard and cheerfully and is popular with her colleagues. Livy comes top in the book-keeping exams and takes a job in the accounts department in the offices of the local county council. Her work is more pedestrian, her fellow workers staid, and she often envies Emmy the camaraderie which exists at the hotel. Because they are living at home, their relationship continues to be undermined by Rosie but they enjoy the occasional lunch hour together. Things settle down and Livy and Em make new friends. They regularly go dancing and to the cinema with this group of young people and the bond between the two sisters grows strong again.

The following year, Liv becomes engaged to a recently qualified young doctor who has joined the practice in the town. It is a whirlwind romance; love at first sight for them both. He is very serious and very devoted and very possessive. Mo is thrilled and begins to make plans for the wedding. Fa, relieved to see Livy with the prospect of a secure, comfortable life ahead of her, is persuaded to put down a deposit for a tiny flat as an engagement present. Excited to be the joint owner of such a charming little dwelling, Liv decides to leave home and move into the flat at once. Mo is reluctant to let her go – it seems, somehow, to foreshadow the end of an era – but Livy is not to be talked out of it. She is, as she points out, only a short bus ride away. At last they agree, although it is to be clearly understood that the young doctor is not to join her until after the nuptials. The town is small enough – and local mouths big enough – to guarantee that the engaged couple behave in accordance with Fa's wishes but Emmy drops in regularly to help out with the refurbishing and to chat.

Envious of Liv's freedom and independence, Emmy makes her own plans to leave home. She has begun to find the difficulties of working shifts irksome and so she decides to live-in at the hotel. This time Mo raises no objections; she is relieved to think of Emmy and Liv within five minutes of each other. The sisters begin to spend even more time together and, one evening, they dream up a plan to go to the big city for a last fling before Liv becomes a respectable married woman. They decide that it is wise not to tell Liv's young doctor about their prospective weekend away and she tells him that she and Em are going to the wedding of a former schoolfriend.

The 'fling' is an enormous success. By accident they meet up with two boyfriends from earlier days and have tremendous fun. The following weekend, Liv and Emmy go home for Mo's birthday. They spend hours in Liv's bedroom reliving the events of their 'fling', giggling away together just as they did in the happy days before the party. Neither of them has much to say to Rosie. During their absence she has purloined several of their most treasured belongings and carried them away to her room. They take her to task although they try to keep it from Mo, since it is her birthday. Rosie is obliged to return the things and, when Livy sees that a little china box – saved from the days of the actress – is cracked, she loses her temper and smacks Rosie soundly.

Rosie does not report this to Mo and Fa – Mo has forbidden her to touch the girls' things – but, a week later, the young doctor receives an anonymous letter detailing the events of the 'fling'. Names and places are mentioned and, when he confronts Livy with this damning evidence, she is too shocked to deny it. Betrayed and angry, he breaks off the engagement and Livy is humiliated and very miserable. She truly loves her young doctor.

'Who could have told him?' moans Liv. 'Who?'

'We must have been seen,' reasons Em. 'Some bloody troublemaker or other.'

'I can't stay here,' weeps Liv. 'I shall see him nearly every day. He cuts me dead. Everyone's talking. Oh, what shall I do? What shall I tell Mo and Fa? Suppose they find out what we did?'

'It wasn't *that* bad,' says Em bitterly. 'Tell you what. Why don't we both move away? Get jobs in London? We could share a flat.'

Liv stares at her, hope making a tentative come-back. 'Could we?'

'Why not?' shrugs Emmy. 'It's getting boring here and Fa will drone on about the money for the deposit.'

'Oh God . . .'

'He can sell the flat,' says Em callously.

Mo is horrified and Fa is furious. Livy is accused of ingratitude and light-mindedness and voices are raised and doors slammed. Rosie moves through the house on light feet, her lips curved in a smile. Em supports Livy staunchly and tries to protect her from Mo's reproach and Fa's indignation. Livy is too unhappy to defend herself and longs to get away, weeping herself to sleep each night and moping in her bedroom by day. In desperation, Em contacts an old school chum in London who tells them that they can stay at her flat until they have found jobs and lodgings. A few weeks later, the girls have gone.

Liv never really gets over her doctor. Despite a new job in a west-end store and the business of flat-hunting and making new friends, she cannot forget him; nor does she cease to brood on who has betrayed her. A few months later, she writes to him from London, pleading with him to be reasonable and assuring him that nothing has happened, but his pride is badly damaged and he is too young to be reasonable. She meets other young men but somehow they never quite measure up and she vows that she will remain a spinster. Emmy, meanwhile, is introduced to a lawyer who works in a big City firm. He is kind and thoughtful but fun, too, and Emmy falls in love with him very quickly. Since his parents have recently emigrated to New Zealand, Emmy invites him home for Christmas to meet Mo and Fa. He accepts with great alacrity and the three of them arrive on Christmas Eve, laden down with presents and prepared for fun.

Everything is ready; the long curtains drawn against the cold, a roaring log fire in the drawing room and a tall Christmas tree in the hall. Fa has restocked the cellar and has concocted one of Pamela's cocktails. There are huggings and kissings and introductions; the lights on the tree are switched on and the parcels piled beneath its tinsel-laden boughs. Rosie, tall and long-legged and looking more than her fourteen years, smiles demurely at the lawyer and kisses her sisters with touching affection. She flits about fetching and carrying and making herself useful – and conspicuous. She has not been sent away to school; Mo and Fa can't bear to part with their Little Princess and Rosie has no intention of allowing herself to become dispensable.

This little ray of sunshine dances to and fro on her long

legs, one eye on the lawyer. The whole party attend Midnight Mass – even Rosie, who has been confirmed this summer dressed in virginal white – all of them squashing into Fa's car. By the end of the service Rosie is nearly asleep, she stumbles as they come out into the freezing air and Emmy bundles her into the car, depositing her on the lawyer's lap and then climbing in afterwards. Rosie, feigning sleep, nestles artlessly close, skirt riding high over the long legs. The lawyer smiles at Emmy, anxiously willing away certain treacherous sensations. Rosie wriggles her tight little backside into his crotch and he shuts his eyes and tries to concentrate on the conversation going on around him.

When they arrive home, Rosie is prettily embarrassed to wake up on his lap. She makes rather too much fuss about it, elaborately pulling down her skirt and bridling with maidenly modesty as she watches him from beneath her lashes. Em, who is tired, snaps at her impatiently.

'Don't be so silly,' she says. 'You're only a little girl. Stop showing off and go to bed.'

The lawyer laughs nervously and, mortified, Rosie hurries away. The girls and Mo make tea in the kitchen whilst the lawyer stands with Fa by the fire and drinks a large Scotch very quickly. He feels unsettled by the incident and is relieved to see Emmy smiling at him happily as she carries the tray into the drawing room.

Christmas Day passes in a haze of goodwill and it is not until Boxing Day that Rosie is given the chance for which she has been watching and waiting. Everybody, except Rosie, drinks too much at lunchtime. Emmy retires to bed to sleep it off and Livy and Fa go out for a walk whilst Mo fiddles quietly in the kitchen, listening to the radio. The lawyer, unused to such quantities and mixtures of alcohol, dozes on the sofa before the fire in the drawing room. When Rosie sinks down beside him, he opens his eyes with difficulty. His head is swimming a little and his tongue feels several sizes too large for his mouth.

'Hello young Rosie,' he mumbles. 'How's . . . how're . . . things?' He tries to focus his eyes and laughs happily. 'Lovely . . . lovely Chriss . . . Chrissmuss.' He gives up and lets his head fall back on the cushions.

'Have you enjoyed it?' She edges closer and lays a hand on his chest.

He squints down at the hand and lays his own hand on top of it. She giggles and carries his arm round her waist, kneeling beside him, her hair tickling his nose. She shoulders in, so that her small breasts press against his chest.

'Are you drunk?' she asks.

He chuckles. He feels contented and relaxed, confident that Fa will approve when he asks for Em's hand in marriage later on that evening. Happiness washes over him and he tightens his grip on Emmy's little sister.

'You can be bridesmaid,' he says. 'Give us a kiss, sis.'

He laughs at his silly little joke and, as he clumsily kisses Rosie's face, his other hand somehow gets entangled in Rosie's legs and is trapped between her knees. Her screams restore him to a fuddled sobriety and he stares up in alarm at Mo who has come racing in from the kitchen. Rosie, having made certain that Mo has seen all the damning evidence, flings herself into her arms, sobbing violently. Fa, just back from his walk, hears the terrible accusations from a barely coherent Mo and a sobbing Rosie. The lawyer, head reeling, is not allowed to explain and what, after all, could he say with Mo calling him terrible names and Rosie in tears? Who would believe him?

'Think yourself lucky,' says Fa, trembling with fury, 'that I don't report you to the Law Society.'

After that there is nothing more to say. In silence Fa drives the white-faced lawyer to the hotel and leaves him on the steps, Rosie is given a sedative and tucked up in bed and it is left to Mo to tell Emmy that her lover is a child molester.

'I don't believe it!' shouts Emmy, shocked. 'He's not *like* that!'

'I *saw* him,' says Mo, white-faced, and is obliged to describe the scene to a disbelieving Emmy.

'It's not true,' she weeps. 'There's some terrible mistake.'

The next morning, Rosie is silent and withdrawn but shakes her head bravely when Mo suggests that they call the doctor. Emmy can hardly bring herself to look at her little sister and is confused by her emotions.

The whole family is shattered by the incident and Christmas is ruined.

Livy and Em return to London. Without the doctor and the lawyer their lives seem empty and they are glad of each other's company. Emmy is still unable to come to terms with what has happened and cannot understand why she should hate Rosie more than the lawyer. For a while she believes that she will hear from him; that by some miracle all will be put right, although she cannot imagine how. The months pass, however, and there is no word from him, no explanation, and she is obliged to attempt to forget him.

Liv has a relationship with a married man, which comes to nothing, and embarks on a rather erratic affair with a divorced journalist who has a caustic tongue and a taste for whisky. With Livy out so much, Emmy grows more and more lonely. She begins to date a widower, with two children almost as old as herself, and is grateful for his solicitous but undemanding company.

As Rosie grows up she occasionally goes to stay with her sisters who include her in their social life and introduce her to their friends. At a party given by one of Em's chums, the eligible stockbroker – who has been invited for Em – falls passionately in love with her little sister. He pursues her with flattering gifts of flowers and chocolates. Rosie sees at once that he is everything that she has ever desired; rich, handsome, unscrupulous, besotted. She plays him with consummate skill and lands him with ease. Mo and Fa are ecstatic that she should have made such a conquest and encourage the match without restraint. Rupert is welcomed and fêted as though he is the Prodigal Son. The ring is chosen and the church booked; they are to be married two months after Rosie's nineteenth birthday.

Livy and Em panic. They imagine the comments at the wedding; the pitying glances of friends and relations. They see themselves walking down the aisle after a radiant Rosie, two thirty-year-old bridesmaids behind the child bride, and imagine they will hear the phrase 'left on the shelf' being whispered behind their backs. Unable to face such shame, Emmy quickly agrees to marry the widower and Livy accepts a proposal from the journalist, made whilst he is in his cups. Mo is terribly disappointed to see her two beautiful daughters throwing themselves away on such men. To her dismay, both weddings are to take place at registry offices and, when she meets the two men, it is clear to her that real love is not present in either of these transactions. The widower is the same age as Fa and very set in his ways; the journalist has a roving eye and his speech is slurred.

'I'm terribly worried about the girls,' she tells Fa.

'Is Jessie Matthews still alive?' he asks.

'Martin is far too quiet for a lively girl like Em,' says Mo, crossly. 'And Bill is a bad lot if you ask me.'

'*Is* anyone asking you?' Fa is wondering how on earth he can afford the kind of wedding Mo and Rosie are planning without going bankrupt and is only too pleased that Emmy and Liv are having quiet ceremonies without any cost to himself. 'They are quite old enough to know their own minds,' he grunts, rustling the *Daily Telegraph*.

'Thirty is a very difficult age,' says Mo, anxiously.

Fa raises his newspaper and, behind the sheets, begins to sob very quietly to himself.

# 6

Mo is absolutely right. Martin *is* very set in his ways; he is, however, comfortably placed in a terraced house at Richmond and his children – grown up now with children of their own – are settled; both sons in Canada. He is the headmaster of a local primary school and, once they are married, he insists that Emmy gives up her job and becomes a lady of leisure. It is faintly shocking to him that his wife should go out to work – 'a woman's place is in the home' – although she is allowed to do Good Works. Emmy is not particularly upset about the job, which was fairly boring, but does not take readily to Good Works. The friends of his late middle-aged wife are quite a lot older and faintly hostile to this new young wife. Might she not give their husbands dangerous ideas? Tweeded and pearled, they regard her button-through maxi-skirt and knee-high leather boots with something like alarm.

Emmy begins to spend more and more time at home, staring out of windows and drinking coffee she doesn't want, trying to find a job which won't interfere with Martin's long school holidays. He is a great walker; coastal paths and Scottish hills; open moors and hidden rights-of-way; none is safe from his booted feet. Em pants along behind him, thinking of those happy lazy days with Liv in the London flat, when rigorous exercise meant walking down two flights to get the milk and running for the bus each weekday morning.

Livy fares worse. Bill *is* a bad lot. He drinks heavily so that his work suffers. He fails to meet his deadlines and their life becomes a flight from small flat to yet smaller flat whilst the debts mount behind them. There is no question of Liv giving up work; in fact she has two jobs. By day she works in the accounts department of the large west end store; by night she works in a coffee bar. No sooner does she fall into bed than it is time to rise and start all over again. There is no question of holidays but she, too, remembers with affection those days with Emmy in the flat.

They lunch together regularly but soon give up any form of intercourse between the four of them. When Livy and Bill are invited to dinner it is a disaster. Bill, who has already drunk quite a lot before they set out, makes insultingly witty remarks about Martin's middle-class way of life, drinks a great deal more during the evening and is sick in the front garden on his way out. Martin is disgusted, although he is sorry for Livy, and tells Emmy that it is clear that he and Bill are not destined to be friends. Emmy helps Liv financially whenever she can, gives her clothes she pretends she doesn't want and worries about her.

Neither of them likes Rupert. He is ten years older than Rosie; careful to the point of meanness; complacent; greedy. He always seems to be eating; sneaking a chocolate from a box, peanuts from dishes, the shavings from the carved joint, the crumbs from the cake plate. He picks continually; slipping into the larder to gulp down some goodie or snatching a biscuit from the tin whilst no one is looking. By Emmy's standards – and certainly by Livy's – he is wealthy. He is also tall and conventionally good-looking and feels that Rosie's English-rose beauty and her charming ways will be an excellent foil for him. His parents adore her. Before he finally commits himself he takes her to meet his boss – even his passion doesn't quite cloud his sense of priorities – and is relieved to have his approval.

Livy and Em call him Roop because he hates it and they refuse to be matrons of honour. Rosie, smiling sweetly, agrees that, given their age, their decision is probably wise and chooses two, rather plain, school-friends. Roop puts the girls' abrasive behaviour down to jealousy and Rosie hastens to encourage this idea. She tells him that Emmy is in love with him and is furious that he has rejected her in favour of her little sister. She explains that Em has married Martin so that no one should guess her true feelings and begs that Roop must be tolerant, to show poor Emmy affection, to ignore her rudeness which is merely a cover for her adoration.

Roop, who is a bigot, has no difficulty in believing that Emmy is in love with him and infuriates her by giving her patronising pats, roaring with laughter at her cutting insults and winking privately at her across the dinner-table. Each time he kisses Rosie, he has one eye on Em.

Rosie excuses Livy's antipathy by explaining to Roop that she is a lesbian. He must be kind to the poor thing, insists Rosie. Her disastrous marriage to Bill is merely a camouflage for her perversions. See how she is always dressed in jeans and has her hair cut so short, whispers Rosie to the shocked Roop. She tells him that, even as a child, Livy preferred to wear shorts and insisted on cropped hair. Rosie invents the story of some fuss at school which nearly resulted in Liv's expulsion but explains that he must never, ever, even *hint* that she has told him about it. Poor Mo and Fa have suffered quite enough as it is and would be humiliated if they thought that Roop knew the truth. He must never, never let poor Livy know that he suspects but must show her great affection, whatever her reaction might be.

Roop is the sort of man who believes that a woman is a lesbian only because she's never been lucky enough to

have sex with the proper man and he even goes so far
as to wonder how he might be able to put Livy right. He
flaunts himself before her, hugs her at every opportunity,
and tells her how pretty she'd look if only she'd let her hair
grow a little.

Liv is almost speechless with rage; almost. 'He is *insuffer-
able*,' she cries.

'If he pats me once more,' rages Em, 'I shall sock him one.
I shall *kill* him.'

Truly, she speaks prophetically.

The years pass. Martin makes it quite clear that, having done
his duty as a father, he has no intention of having any more
children. He is too old to start again with nappies and bottles
and disturbed nights. Em, who feels that she would like a
child so long as it isn't Martin's, accepts his decision. She
brushes up on her typing and takes in work to do at home.
Her life is unfulfilled but placid enough and she occasionally
wonders how it might have been if she had married the
lawyer. Martin is relatively undemanding, although he likes
order and regularity in the running of his home, but when
Em compares her existence to Liv's she realises that she is
very fortunate.

When Liv becomes pregnant through carelessness, Bill
insists that she has an abortion. How, he demands, can
they possibly afford a child? How can they survive if Liv
stops working? He knows someone who is perfectly safe and
respectable who can do the job . . . Liv, in their depressing
little bedsit, is worn down and exhausted, nevertheless she
longs to keep her baby. Common sense, however, shows her
what kind of future it could expect and she weeps bitterly in
private and borrows the money from Em.

Rosie, in the comfort of Roop's house in Chelsea, lives
in a whirl of parties and fun. Although she and Roop
plan to have a family they decide to wait a little longer.

After all, Rosie is so young and Roop is still 'establishing' himself . . .

'Establishing himself as what?' asks Livy waspishly of Em.
 'The biggest prick in London,' replies Emmy.

Mo is disappointed that Livy and Em have not yet produced children. She can understand that Martin is old and that Bill is poor, nevertheless she longs to hold her grandchildren in her arms.
 'Children are such a blessing,' she says wistfully to Fa.
 'Is Mrs Dale a grandmother yet?' asks Fa. To pay for Rosie's wedding he has had to remortgage the house and he is wondering if he will ever be able to afford to retire. He has pains in his chest and gets dizzy when he runs upstairs. He has had a letter from Liv asking if he can help her pay three months' back rent.
 'Of course the late thirties is a difficult age to have children,' says Mo thoughtfully.
 'And the twenties,' shouts Fa, 'and the forties and the fifties and the sixties. Dear Christ! when *isn't* a difficult age to have bloody children?'

Rosie is having such a wonderful time that she postpones motherhood for yet a few more years. Roop's friends are nearly ten years older than she is and they pet and spoil her. Liv and Emmy rarely visit her. Roop is able to understand that it must be sheer hell for Em to see him so happy as Rosie's husband but nevertheless he feels it keenly that Rosie is unable to enjoy her sisters' envy of the worldly goods that pack the Chelsea house. Livy and Em have done the conducted tour shortly after the honeymoon; standing before some antique piece of furniture or rare painting whilst Roop explains at length how he got it by driving a hard bargain, doing someone down or obtaining it by some other method for which he considers that he deserves praise. The usual sycophantic replies – 'You don't say so!' 'I don't believe it!' 'God, you're a hard man!' – are conspicuously absent when he shows Livy and Em round the house.

They stand in silence, staring indifferently at Roop's achievements. Roop is the kind of person whose belongings are only truly of value to him if they are admired and coveted by others – and especially by those less fortunate than he is. He begins to give a greater history of each object, its age and market value, its rarity and beauty. When Livy and Em remain unimpressed, he starts on the value of the house and the desirability of its position. Presently he pauses, so as to give them time to admire and envy . . .

'Do two people really *need* four lavatories?' asks Liv.

'It depends how full of shit the people are,' replies Em.

Rosie reminds the puzzled and disappointed Roop of Emmy's unrequited love for him, of Liv's unwomanly tendencies, and of the well-disguised jealousy of both for the wonderful things that she and Roop own. He is mollified but frustrated.

When she is twenty-five, Rosie gives birth. She has a difficult pregnancy and a prolonged labour and decides that this is an experience which she will never repeat. She and the baby go to stay with Mo so as to give Rosie time to recover. Mo is thrilled. Rosie is more than content to sit on the terrace, relaxing on a sun-bed, whilst Mo happily looks after the baby. She has already prepared the crib and the Silver Cross pram and knitted new blankets and little jackets with booties to match.

'Just think,' Mo says dreamily, 'I was pushed along this terrace in this pram. And so was Emmy and so were you. Isn't it lovely to think of that?'

Rosie opens one eye and yawns. 'Riveting,' she says.

'I was wondering,' says Mo, not attending, 'whether you'd

like to take it back to London with you. After all, no one else is going to want it. I'd love to think that you were using it.'

'Sweet of you,' says Rosie, readjusting a cushion, 'but we've already got one. Mother bought it for us. And the sweetest little crib.'

Mo is silent. It hurts to hear Rosie using the word 'mother'. It is years, well, twenty-seven, to be exact, since Mo has been called mummy or mother and she feels a strange sense of loss. Rosie glances up, alerted by the silence.

'Well, after all,' she points out, 'it would be very difficult to get such a big pram back to London. It wouldn't fit in the car. That's why Mother bought us a new one. Rupert's was too big, too.'

'I suppose,' says Mo bravely, 'that it's sensible to keep it here, ready for when you visit with Baby. You must decide on a name for her soon, darling. It's so important that she has her own identity.'

'Mmm,' says Rosie, feigning sleep. She and Roop have already decided that the baby will be called Alice after his mother. The money in Roop's family comes from his mother's side and they don't want to risk upsetting her. Roop's sister has been asked to be godmother and the baby's second name will be Susan in compliment to her. Rosie is feeling a little guilty at the exclusion of her own family but has no intention of asking either Liv or Emmy to be the other godmother, nor of adding the name Maureen to Alice Susan. She does, however, want to have the baby baptised in the thirteenth-century village church.

Mo is delighted and terrified in turn. Roop's family must be accommodated and she has no intention of letting the side down. Several bedrooms have to be redecorated and new rugs bought. The house is full to bursting point and friends have to be put up in the local pub. It all goes without a hitch, however, and even Emmy and Liv make a tremendous effort to be polite to Roop. He sees their politeness as a reaffirmation of desire, imagining that even Livy is unable to withstand his charms, and his complacency is abominable. He is able to gorge himself and, even after the enormous lunch, is unable to resist nipping into the larder to pinch the remaining cherries off the trifle.

Mo is relieved that it all passes off successfully, but she is hurt by Rosie's treachery at calling the baby after Roop's mother and sister and refusing to allow either Livy or Em to be a godparent. For once she is unmoved by Rosie's attempts to wheedle her and a coolness develops. Several months pass and, when Rosie and Roop next visit, Mo sees great changes in the baby. She whines and cries all the day long, only happy if she is being danced in someone's arms or being fed. Mo is convinced that Alice is being spoilt. It appears that Roop's mother and sister are for ever staying at the Chelsea house and Mo sees at once where the danger lies. She decides to open Rosie's eyes and, just before they return to London, warns her against her in-laws.

There is an unpleasant little scene and Mo is left to have a private little weep. She is not feeling so good these days and is prone to headaches and spells of depression. Fa is no help, being constantly preoccupied and rather short-tempered. Next morning, however, she broaches the subject.

'I'm terribly worried about Alice,' she says, passing him the cornflakes.

'Pity she wasn't a boy,' he says morosely. 'We could have called him Jim.'

'She never stopped crying the whole time she was here,' says Mo, gritting her teeth. 'But naturally Rosie won't hear a word against Roop's mother. I've a good mind to have a word with her myself. It's not good for young parents to have in-laws in the house all the time. I think I have a right to my opinion. Alice is our grandchild as well as theirs. We have a responsibility towards her . . .'

'Unfortunately,' puts in Fa, resentfully. 'As far as I'm concerned,' he adds callously, 'they're welcome to her.'

He has had to borrow the money to pay for the christening party from a colleague who is now pressing for payment. The friends who stayed at the pub forgot to pay their bill and the decorator's account has just arrived.

'How can you say such a thing?' asks Mo, shocked.

Suddenly the pressure is simply too much to bear. 'These bloody girls have *ruined* me,' he cries. 'You've catered to their every whim and if we have to sell this house to make ends meet it will be *your* fault.'

She stares at him in amazement and self-pity sweeps over her, along with a surge of fury. 'How *dare* you speak to me like that,' she cries. 'I, who have supported and looked after you all these years and brought up your daughter as though she were my own. Don't think,' she shouts unfairly, 'that I have not noticed your grudging attitude towards *my* daughter whilst you have lived here in my family's house nor,' she hisses, 'that I have been unaware of your ridiculous obsession with Jessie Matthews. Nevertheless, I feel that even you might realise that I am not as young as I was.' She gives a loud sob. 'You might have noticed, if you stopped thinking about yourself for a few moments, that I am at a *very difficult age*!'

Fa gives a great roar of frustrated rage. He leaps to his feet . . . and falls dead amongst the breakfast things.

# 7

Pamela appears at Fa's funeral. Divorced three times, thin to the point of gauntness, a long silk scarf twined about the scraggy neck, she is, nevertheless, the same old Pamela. After the baked meats have been eaten, Roop having disposed of three times as much as anyone else, she sees everyone off the premises with the ruthlessness of a bouncer at a nightclub. Mo is listless, apathetic and withdrawn. Emmy and Liv have arranged everything and feel they should stay with her but Pamela persuades them to return to London. She assures them that she will stay with Mo; that Mo needs time to recover quietly. They will be needed when she, Pamela, has to return to the States. Livy and Em give in reluctantly. Martin has to get back for school the next day; Bill, owing to a colossal hangover, has not even attended. Rosie and Roop have already left.

Pamela closes the front door with relief and goes back to Mo, who is in the drawing room . . .

'What we need, hon,' she says, prowling about the room like a lean old wolf, 'is a *real* drink. Where d'you keep it?'

Mo, huddled in an armchair, opens her eyes wearily. 'Dining room,' she says succinctly. 'Sideboard.'

Pamela bounds away and returns, clinking. The tray she carries is packed with bottles and includes two glasses. There are sounds of gluggings and swooshings as Pamela pours and mixes.

'Here,' she says, standing over the supine Mo. 'Get yourself outside that.'

Mo shrinks a little in her chair. 'I don't really drink,' she murmurs. 'No. Really.'

'Sure you do,' bullies Pamela. 'It's a pick-me-up. It'll do you good. Ed wouldn't want you going to pieces.'

At the sound of Fa's name – abbreviated with such easy familiarity – Mo stirs, as though she hears a distant trumpet summoning her to the fray. She remembers how she disliked Pamela in those far off days. Other memories stir; how she privately ridiculed Fa, dwelling spitefully on his bald patch and his laugh; the longing she had to hit him with something hard with knobs on . . . Remorse seizes her.

'Oh, Pamela,' she moans. 'He was such a good man. So kind and generous.'

'Sure he was,' drawls Pamela. 'Here. Let's drink to him.'

Snivelling, Mo takes the glass. 'Fa,' she says – and sips.

'Ed,' says Pamela – and gulps. 'He was one great guy.'

Mo's lips quiver. She remembers her last accusations across the breakfast table and is unable to contain her grief. 'Waaaagh,' she wails.

Pamela lays back in her chair, sipping and smoking whilst Mo keens. 'Let it all hang out,' she says comfortably. 'Don't hold back. Drink up, hon. It'll make you feel better.'

Between wails, Mo sips. Presently she begins to feel less miserable; a glow is spreading through her frame. Pamela refills their glasses.

'It helps to mourn,' says Mo much later, stifling a hiccup.

'Sure it does,' agrees Pamela. 'And it helps to drink. Let's have another.'

'Well,' says Mo, giggling a little. 'Well, I'm not sure. Should we . . . ?'

'Sure we should,' says Pamela, pouring. 'Just you trust your Auntie Pammie.'

The afternoon and evening pass. The two women lie

recumbent in their chairs, moving only to refill their glasses. At some point they rise unsteadily and stagger upstairs. Mo shows Pamela to her room.

'I once found my mother in this very bed,' she says, enunciating carefully, 'awash with gin.'

'Izzat so?' Pamela focuses with difficulty upon the piece of furniture in question. 'Awash?'

'She was seventy years old,' says Mo proudly.

Pamela shakes her head admiringly – and winces a little. 'You don't say so? Awash with gin at seventy years old? That's some lady.' She falls headlong upon the bed and remains, comatose.

'She was a very great lady,' slurs Mo. She feels, at this moment, the shade of her mother close at hand, comforting her as she feels her way to her own room. 'Mother?' she murmurs, as she climbs into bed, fully clothed.

As she spirals into sleep she is vouchsafed a vision. She sees Mother and Fa in some distant Elysian field, gambolling together. Her mother is holding a glass. They are both now looking towards her, saluting her. Mo remembers a toast that Pamela has used at intervals during the evening. She smiles and tries to raise her arm, her fingers clutching a non-existent glass.

'Here's looking at you, kid,' she mutters.

Pamela stays one week, then two, then a month. A year later she is still living with Mo. Fa's death has solved most of the financial problems but there is no income for Mo. He has gradually sold up all his stocks and shares and cashed in his insurance policies, except the one which secured the house and paid off the mortgage.

'Thank God I have a roof over my head,' says Mo. 'But how shall I live?'

'Just trust your Auntie Pammie,' says Pamela, who has an income from her three ex-husbands, but no home. 'Now just you go on out in that sunshine and do some weeding. I'm going to do some Serious Shopping.'

Mo knows by now that Serious Shopping is not for the fundamentals of life – bread, milk, eggs and so on – but for booze and cigarettes. She has long since ceased to worry about it. The little nips she shares with Pamela at intervals through the day hold grief and anxiety at bay. Betty still comes up from the village to help out and she and Mo talk about the old days. Betty has a daughter of her own, now, called Jackie, who sometimes comes with her, and Mo and Betty reminisce together and marvel at how quickly the years pass.

These days Mo is much calmer and is no longer terribly worried about anyone. She talks everything through with Pamela who is a much more satisfying *confidante* than ever Fa was. They discuss Martin's dullness, Bill's selfishness and Roop's greed and Pamela, hoping to protect Livy and Em as far as possible, encourages Mo to make a will dividing her property equally between the three girls. When Pamela has been installed for some months, Mo even broaches the subject of Fa's obsession. It still rankles and she cannot quite bring herself to admit the truth straight out to Pamela.

'Ever heard of Jessie Matthews?' she asks casually.

Pamela frowns. 'Some kinda cowboy, wasn't he?'

Mo decides that she cannot be bothered to pursue it after all. It doesn't seem to matter any more.

The year before he is due to retire, Martin is killed in a car accident in Canada. He has been visiting his sons and, in a moment of aberration, forgets to drive on the right-hand side of the road. Emmy flies out for the funeral, since it has been decided that Martin should be buried close to his family. He has been scrupulously fair when it comes to the division of his possessions but it is clear that, if she wishes to survive financially, Emmy must sell the house at Richmond so as to live on the proceeds.

Whilst Em is wondering what to do and where to go, Livy discovers that Bill has been having a long-standing affair with another woman. Without a moment's hesitation, she collects her few belongings and walks out. She goes to Emmy and they sit together in Emmy's kitchen.

'The bastard!' says Em. 'The absolute and utter bastard. You've been supporting him for fifteen years.'

'Gave him plenty of opportunity, didn't I?' says Liv bitterly. 'Out all day. Out all evening. I wondered where the money was going. All that bloody effort.'

'And the baby,' says Emmy sadly. 'Oh, Liv . . .'

'Forget it,' says Liv. 'It's over. Should've done it years ago. It was just pride I suppose. Couldn't bear to admit I've failed. Can you imagine Rosie's reaction? Oh, I can't face it!'

'We'll think of something,' promises Emmy. 'We won't give her the satisfaction of knowing what's happened. Trust me.'

'You sound like Pamela,' says Liv morosely.

'Listen,' says Em. 'Why don't we go down and see them. Pamela and Mo, I mean. It's really jolly down there these days. Let's give ourselves time to regroup. I've got to sell up. You've got to think about your future. Take a few days off.'

'I've given in my notices,' says Liv with a show of bravado. 'Both of them.'

'Good for you,' says Emmy, sensing terror beneath Liv's defiance. 'We'll manage somehow. Come on. Let's go home.'

The house, standing on the hill above the village, seems to welcome them. The mellowed brick glows warmly in the evening sun. The clematis is in full flower and the windows are lit as if by tongues of flame. A table is set on the terrace with chairs grouped about it and Mo and

Pamela rise to greet the girls as they climb stiffly from
Emmy's little car.

'Welcome. Welcome,' cries Pamela as Mo hurries to
embrace them.

'Darlings,' she says – Emmy has warned her about Liv –
'oh, how lovely to have you home. Come and sit down and
have a drink before dinner.'

Livy and Em allow themselves to be fussed over and spoilt.
They feel that they are children again, to be loved and petted,
and they push aside their fears and disappointments and
relax into the warmth. Their rooms are ready for them
with their old toys and books still ranged about the walls
and, when they meet on the landing after a quick wash and
brush up, they smile at each other.

'Good to be back, isn't it?' says Em.

'It's funny,' says Livy. 'We couldn't wait to get away – but
for the life of me I can't remember why.'

'I can,' says Em grimly. 'Darling, bloody Rosie. That's
why.'

Like Pamela, Emmy and Liv find it difficult to tear themselves away. Once Livy really begins to relax she has a minor
breakdown.

'Overwork,' says the doctor whom Livy once loved.
'Overwork, stress, poor diet. What has she been up to?'

'Oh,' says Emmy, not wanting to let Livy down. 'Just
trying to survive. You know how it is.'

He is no longer very young, nor is he very serious. He has
been a regular visitor to the house through the whole of one
winter when Pamela was ill and now feels quite at home,
sitting in the kitchen and chatting.

'We'll have to build her up,' he says. 'Complete rest for
the time being.'

Mo and Pamela are very ready to share the care of
the invalid, although Livy takes longer to recover than

everyone expects. By the end of the summer, however, she is beginning to improve. She lies on a steamer chair in the summerhouse in the early autumn sunshine and thinks about the past. She is able to do so now without weeping. The doctor sits with her occasionally, sharing the tea which Mo and Pamela bring out to tempt the convalescent's appetite, and they talk about old times.

Once the house in Richmond sells, it seems natural to Emmy to go back to Mo and Liv and Pamela. She is welcomed by all three.

'This is lovely,' says Mo happily. 'All of us together again. Wouldn't Fa be pleased?'

Rosie and Roop are very concerned by the situation. First Pamela moves in; now Livy and Em seem to be living permanently with Mo.

'I don't like it,' says Roop.

'Why not darling?' asks Rosie. 'Why does it matter where they live? At least it means that we don't have to worry about Mo.'

'We have to think about your part of the inheritance,' says Roop.

They exchange a thoughtful glance.

'There's only the house left,' points out Rosie.

'But think of its position,' exclaims Roop. 'It could be made into several very nice executive flats. There's a great demand for luxury flats in a country setting. Now that they've put the motorway through it's become commuterland. We'd get a fortune for it.'

'But we're in the middle of a recession,' protests Rosie.

Roop laughs. 'Don't worry about that. There are still plenty of people around with money.'

'No harm, then, in waiting,' says Rosie. 'Surely it will be even more desirable in a few years' time? Anyway we can't turn Mo out.'

'True,' agrees Roop. 'But I must check up on the law relating to sitting tenants.'

'Mo isn't a sitting tenant,' argues Rosie.

'Pamela might be,' says Roop grimly. 'Does she pay your mother rent? We can't be too careful. And now it looks as if Livy and Em are digging themselves in.'

'You make it sound like trench warfare,' says Alice, suddenly appearing from the shadowy alcove.

Rosie and Roop look at their fifteen-year-old daughter. She resembles Roop's mother, which is unfortunate, and, like her father, she is greedy. At present, she is overweight and has a skin problem. Rosie and Roop sigh in unison. Alice smiles slyly; she enjoys frustrating their ambitions.

'What's wrong with Livy and Emmy living with Grandmother?'

'Never you mind,' says Rosie sharply. It hurts her that she has produced such an unattractive daughter, 'And don't go saying anything next time we're there.'

Once or twice Rosie and Roop have been dropped in it by Alice's devastatingly innocent comments and it would be unfortunate if Rosie's family were to realise that they are sitting on a gold mine. Alice raises her eyebrows provocatively and purses her lips thoughtfully. Roop and Rosie exchange another glance.

'Wasn't there some party you were going to?' Roop asks his daughter casually. 'Didn't I hear something . . .'

'Ma says I can't,' says Alice sulkily – but her eyes dart brightly between the two of them. 'She's got this thing about drugs . . .'

'There are no grown-ups supervising it,' explains Rosie quickly. 'I'm only trying to protect her.'

'Quite,' says Roop. 'Very understandable. But I'm sure we can trust Alice to be sensible. If we put her on her honour . . .'

'I promise,' says Alice. 'Honest. I'll be really careful. And I won't say anything to Livy and Em about Ma's inheritance and what you were saying about luxury flats. I swear I won't.'

They exchange another look.

'In that case,' says Roop, 'if Mummy agrees . . .'

'Very well,' says Rosie. 'But remember that you are on your honour.'

# 8

They are known in the village as the Coven. Four women and three cats, named Freeman, Hardy and Willis, are bound to be of interest. Despite Betty's loyal denials, the villagers talk in low voices about the quantity of alcohol that is carried up to the house; that and the fact that Livy has had a nervous breakdown. The old gossip about her broken engagement is trawled up from the mud and given an airing. Sharp eyes notice how often the doctor's car passes through the village and up the long drive to the house and a scare is put about, the essence of which is that Mo has been done away with so that the other three can get their hands on her property. They are almost disappointed when they see Mo, riding in the car with Emmy, and new stories have to be invented. The doctor begins to hear the whispers and becomes uneasy.

'What is this I hear,' asks his wife, sharp-nosed, glinty-eyed, 'about you and Livy Faringdon?'

'I've no idea,' he says with an insouciance he does not feel. 'What *have* you heard about me and Livy Faringdon?'

'Don't try to be clever with me,' snaps his wife. 'I've heard the stories. Up there all hours. Tea in the summerhouse.'

'She's my patient,' he explains with exaggerated patience. 'She's had a nervous breakdown. So her mother gives me a cup of tea. What am I supposed to do? Throw it in her face?'

The note of guilt which all good wives are able to detect

by day two of the honeymoon, alerts her. So the rumours are true.

'I'm not surprised she's had a nervous breakdown,' she says. 'It must be exhausting, pursuing other women's husbands.'

'I am surprised and disappointed,' he says, taking a high moral tone, 'to hear you descending to this level of gossip. I had hoped that you were above small-town whispering.'

'Don't be a pompous prick,' she says. 'I haven't forgotten the things you told me about her.'

The doctor is silent. He remembers how, in his hurt and humiliation, he poured out the story of the 'fling' to the girl who is now his wife. She was sweet and womanly and sympathetic; shocked by such wanton behaviour; ready to comfort and console. He remembers, too, that, excited by the comforting and soothing, he painted Livy rather blacker than was warranted and how she of the pointy nose and glinty eyes listened avidly, hastening to reassure him that all women were not as Livy Faringdon. She reassured him into an engagement ring, into bed and into church. When they came down the aisle together, man and wife, she was still reassuring him.

'Livy Faringdon,' he says at last, 'is a middle-aged woman who has had a difficult life and is now having a minor nervous breakdown. She is thin and going grey and there is no more between us than is between any doctor and his patient.'

For the present there is nothing more to be said. The doctor treads warily; his wife watches and listens even more carefully. Livy is quite ignorant of these undercurrents and continues to look forward to his visits. She still feels rather weak and is grateful for any show of caring. The winter draws on and Pamela is subject once again to another bout of bronchitis, following the flu which they have all had in turn. The doctor has a perfectly legitimate reason to visit the house and have tea in the study with Livy and Mo and Emmy.

'The trouble was,' Liv tells Emmy, one afternoon whilst he is examining Pamela with Mo in attendance, 'I never really stopped loving him. I married Bill because I couldn't bear to have Rosie pulling rank about being married first. After all, she's ten years younger. It was so humiliating.'

'You and me both,' says Em. 'I just happened to be luckier with Martin, that's all.'

'Well,' Livy shrugs. 'Too late now. Still, it's nice to see him.'

'I think he still cares about you,' says Emmy gently. 'You can see it when he looks at you.'

Liv gives a snort of disbelief, but she looks pleased. Mo reappears and Em hurries out to receive last instructions about Pamela's medicine.

'Liv's looking better,' she says casually.

The doctor frowns. 'Taking longer than it should. She was really pulled down but she's on the mend. Don't let her take any chances. The flu set her back a bit. I might pop in tomorrow to check on Pamela.'

She waves him off thoughtfully. He has given Livy a thorough checkup and has discovered the evidence of a clumsy abortion. At the time, Livy is in no fit state to be questioned so he asks Emmy. She is obliged to explain the circumstances of Liv's life and disastrous marriage – including the abortion – but swears the doctor to secrecy. No one else must know these intimate details; not even Livy knows that Em has told the doctor the truth. Em feels guilty but suspects that it is because he knows how much Liv has suffered that she is getting such care and attention.

All four of them are glad to see the spring and in the summer the girls celebrate their joint fiftieth birthday party. Betty bakes a cake and the doctor arrives with little presents. Pamela mixes an extra special cocktail and for a brief moment they all feel young again.

'But we're not,' says Livy, when the doctor has left and
Pamela and Mo have gone off to prepare a birthday supper for the girls. 'We're fifty. Mo's seventy-two. Pamela's
seventy-five.'

They sit in silence in the summerhouse, staring out. The
rust of the town has corroded the countryside and creeps
ever nearer, threatening to eat up the village.

'Remember when it was all fields?' asks Em.

'It's the motorway I hate,' answers Liv. 'It's never quiet
now. Just the roar of the bloody road all day and all night.'

'It's not that bad,' says Em. 'At least it's a distant roar. If
you shut your eyes you can pretend it's the sea.'

'*You* might be able to,' says Liv, 'but *I* can't. I know it's not
the sea. How can you pretend it's the sea when you can see
the traffic racing along?'

Emmy gazes out towards the motorway. 'Perhaps we
ought to move the summerhouse,' she suggests. 'It's too
high here now the road has been built. We should put it
somewhere so that we can't see it.'

'We'll still hear it though,' grumbles Liv.

There is another silence. Liv is looking at the presents the
doctor has brought; a box of pretty handkerchiefs for Em
and, for Livy, a small bottle of the scent she used to wear
as a girl, Elizabeth Arden's Blue Grass.

'I wonder,' she says, fingering the bottle, 'who sent him
that anonymous letter?'

'Do you know,' asks Rosie, giggling girlishly, 'that down in
the village they call you the Coven? Isn't it a hoot? I thought
that Rupert would die laughing.'

The girls watch her. 'People will say anything,' says Em.

'But still. Too *Macbeth* for words, isn't it? Of course you
can understand why.'

'Can you?' asks Liv.

'Well, really.' Rosie's smile fades. 'Just look at Pamela.

Nothing but an old crone. She's so thin and her eyes are so sunken. And those scarves and shawls she wears. Mad as a hatter. Is she ever sober?'

'Does it matter if she isn't?' asks Em.

'You obviously don't care about her health,' shrugs Rosie. 'She'll die of cirrhosis of the liver if you don't stop her.'

'She's got to die of something,' says Liv. 'Just because death has become a dirty word doesn't mean we can avoid it. At least she's happy.'

'You always take the line of least resistance,' snaps Rosie. 'You're not looking so good yourself.'

'Neither are you,' says Em, 'now you've passed forty. Still going to Weight Watchers?'

'I've never been to Weight Watchers in my life,' cries Rosie angrily. She knows that Alice has been sneaking. 'I've never had a problem with my figure.'

The girls smile.

'Roop's looking his age,' says Em meditatively.

Liv nods. 'Well, he's older than us. Fifty-two? Fifty-three?'

'Getting thin on top and fat round the middle,' says Em. 'All those little treats. Where is he now?'

'In the larder, I expect,' says Liv. 'Sneaking some of the buns that you've made for tea.'

Rosie wills down her anger, swallows her sharp retort and reminds herself that they are jealous. She must regain the upper hand.

'The doctor comes rather a lot, doesn't he?' she asks casually. 'Is there any need for such regular visits?'

She registers the stiffening of Livy's shoulders; the quick clenching of Em's fists.

'Pamela was very ill all last winter,' says Em, rather too quickly. 'As you've already noticed, she's not in the best of health.'

'Still, I shouldn't have thought he needed to come quite so

often.' She pauses, as if for reflection. 'Weren't you engaged to him once?' she asks Liv.

She sees the colour rise in Liv's thin cheeks and notes Em's quick anxious glance at her.

'That's right,' says Liv easily. 'A long time ago.'

'What happened?' asks Rosie, pretending to rack her memory. 'I can't remember. Of course, I was just a child. Did he . . . ?'

'Teatime,' says Emmy, getting up. 'Come on, Liv. Let's hope Roop has left us something to eat.'

Rosie's lips curve in a smile as she watches them go. She feels the time has come for a little detective work. The girls are too close; too loyal. She remembers her old maxim; divide and rule. Roop puts his head in at the door.

'Tea,' he announces, rubbing his hands. 'Lots of lovely cakes. Coming?'

Rosie notices the thinning hair and spreading waistline but she is able to rise above such things. She and Roop are two of a kind; ruled by self-interest; utterly selfish. They are made for each other.

'Give me a kiss first,' she says.

Surprised he obeys, feeling a sense of power which is very pleasant after the jokes the girls have been making at his expense all week.

'Livy looks about eighty,' he whispers in her ear as he runs his hands down over her backside. 'And Pam looks like she's just been dug up. As for those cats . . .'

'The Coven,' Rosie giggles. 'About right, wouldn't you say?'

They laugh immoderately and, arm-in-arm and smug in their superior oneness, they go in to tea together.

Freeman, Hardy and Willis are Persian cats. One day, before Emmy and Liv have come back to live at home, Pam returns from the town, carrying the kittens in her shopping basket.

'Too sweet, hon,' she says, showing Mo. 'Couldn't resist. They were in a cage in the pet shop and this whiny little kid wanted one. I just knew he was a sadist. There was a look about the eyes. I bought all of 'em just so he couldn't have one.'

'Have you known many sadists, Pamela?' asks Mo, interested. In their years together Pamela has thrown a fascinating light on a life Mo has never experienced. 'How do you recognise one so easily?'

'Honey,' says Pam, lifting out the kittens. 'He was a male child. I've had three husbands. I can recognise a sadist at fifty paces.'

'Oh, aren't they sweet?' cries Mo, distracted for a moment from this riveting subject. 'Whatever shall we call them?'

'I thought of that,' says Pamela. 'Coming out of the shop, I thought "Now what are we gonna call these little guys?" And I looked up and guess what I saw?'

'What?' asks Mo, entranced.

'Right across the road was a shop and there were the three names right over the door. "Freeman, Hardy and Willis." And I thought "That's it." Like it was meant to be.'

'They're not very attractive names for such pretty little things,' objects Mo.

'Got a better idea?' asks Pamela easily. 'Can you think of three of anything?'

After a great cudgelling of the brain, all Mo can come up with is Jacksons-Stops and Staff or Knight, Frank and Rutley.

'Perhaps you're right,' she says.

The kittens grow into cats; they are fat and indolent but much beloved. They are too well-fed and too idle to catch birds or chase mice and for this Mo is grateful. She gives them extra titbits as a reward for not bringing corpses into the kitchen as Boswell used to do. As well as the bottles,

Pamela now carts tins and tins of cat food up from the village. Whilst she cooks and drinks and chats to Mo, a cigarette clinging to her lip, the cats weave around her legs, purring, and she intersperses her conversation with words of love and gestures of affection. When Livy and Em move back to live with Mo and Pamela, the cats receive even more attention.

As they grow older, they sleep on Pamela's bed, cuddled around her like a huge furry shawl.

'Honestly,' says Emmy, coming in one morning with a cup of tea and unable to see Pamela for cat. 'Are you in there? Can you breathe? You really do spoil them. They'll be the death of you.'

Truly, she speaks prophetically.

Pamela finds Grandmother's old flask and begins to take it with her to bed, just so as to help her through the night. Her coughing wakes her and then she finds it difficult to go back to sleep. One little pull at the silver chased flask and she is soothed; a few more nips and she is sleepy again. She nestles in with the cats and slumbers peacefully.

One night she wakes with a coughing fit and finds that her flask is almost empty; only a nip or two left. She drains the last drop but there is not enough to create that numbing warmth she craves. She climbs from her bed, huddling into her shawls, and creeps out onto the dark landing. The cats go before her, interested and hopeful. Clutching her flask in one hand and pulling her shawl closer with another, she hesitates at the head of the stairs. Shivering and light-headed she begins to descend. Slowly she creeps down, unsteadily feeling for the next stair with her cold bare toes. She steps on a furry body, loses her precarious balance . . . and goes hurtling down into the blackness of the hall.

# 9

'She wasn't drunk!' weeps Mo. 'She wasn't. She was going down to make herself a hot drink and she fell. She felt the cold so much lately.'

Poor Mo is inconsolable. She cannot believe that Pamela is no more. The doctor gives her a sedative and Emmy tucks her up in bed.

'Does she have to know about the flask?' she asks the doctor.

'No one has to know about the flask,' he tells her. Privately, he is quite certain that Mo has no illusions about Pamela. 'It was dark and she missed her footing. Her neck was broken. Don't worry. Nobody will know.'

Nobody knows but everybody guesses. The rumour is round the village like wildfire. Rosie and Roop come down for the funeral.

'I bet she was drunk,' says Rosie.

'She was not drunk,' says Em steadily. 'She was going down to make herself a hot drink. I think she tripped over one of the cats.'

'What does the doctor say?' asks Roop, his eyes on Liv's face.

'That she broke her neck when she fell,' answers Em, outstaring them. 'And please don't say hurtful things like that to Mo. She's upset enough as it is.'

'Of course, you've got the doctor in the palm of your hand,' says Rosie softly. 'Haven't you?'

'Perhaps we should ask him to give Roop the once over,' suggests Liv. 'You're looking very unhealthy and over-weight, Roop. Thought of taking early retirement?'

When Rosie and Roop drive away after the funeral, Roop is still seething.

'Who cares what they say?' says Rosie. 'Forget it. One down, three to go. And Mo won't last long by the look of it.'

'How Emmy and Liv will hate seeing their old home turned into luxury flats,' says Roop dreamily. 'Strangers on the terrace and in the garden. I can't wait.'

When the funeral is over and everyone gone, Mo sits for-lornly in the drawing room by the fire. She remembers how Pamela cared for her after Fa died and how they mourned together on the evening after his funeral.

'She was my best friend,' she says sadly. 'I never had a friend before Pamela came.'

She weeps a little whilst the girls attempt to comfort her. Liv fetches Freeman – or Hardy – or Willis – and places him on Mo's knee and she cuddles him gratefully.

'I think I should like a drink,' she says to Emmy and Liv.

'Good idea,' says Emmy with relief. The house seems strangely empty without Pamela's gaunt frame drifting from room to room. 'We'll all have one.'

Livy piles logs on to the fire whilst Em goes to fetch the drinks. Watching Mo downing the whisky the girls are faintly impressed.

'I know she has the odd nip,' murmurs Emmy to Liv, 'but I've never seen her put it away quite so quickly.'

'Remember Grandmother and the gin?' asks Liv quietly.

They sit thoughtfully, remembering their grandmother sipping funny smelling water from her flask.

Much later, they assist Mo upstairs and help her into bed. They undress her, tuck her in with her hot-water bottles, kiss her goodnight and retreat quietly towards the door. As she spirals down into sleep, she is vouchsafed a vision. Mother and Fa, gambolling in their Elysian field, have been joined by Pamela. Mother and Pamela are both holding glasses. They are all embracing each other and now they turn towards Mo to salute her. Mo, smiling peacefully, waves back. All her jealousy of Pamela and Fa has evaporated during her years with Pamela. She is glad that Fa is there to welcome her dear old friend; Mother will be able to show her the ropes.

Watching from the door, the girls look at each other, puzzled.

'Who's she waving to?' asks Liv.

'Search me,' says Em.


When she leaves school, Alice is sent down to stay before going off to university. She wants to take a year out but Rosie and Roop won't hear of it.

'We can't afford to have you lolling about for a year,' Roop tells her. 'You can go and spend a few weeks with your Grandmother and aunts in the country.'

'And keep your ears open and your mouth shut,' adds Rosie.

Livy and Em dread the thought of Alice staying but it turns out better than they dare to hope. She sits with Mo, talking with her about the past; or rather Mo talks and Alice listens. She is good at listening; at prompting with a clever question; at sifting the important from the unimportant. She helps with the cooking and the housework and makes herself useful. She has lost weight in her last year at school and she moves lightly and silently; a shadow on the landing catching whispered secrets; a soft footfall in the badly lit corridor by the telephone.

Livy is unwell again. She has stomach pains and heavy periods which hardly ever seem to stop.

'The best thing for her,' says the doctor to Emmy, 'would be a hysterectomy. We'll get her into hospital and give her a good check-up . . .'

'Oh God,' says Emmy, frightened. 'There's nothing really wrong, is there? Is it because of that abortion?'

She glances quickly towards the half-open door. Was that someone outside in the hall? A shadow? The flick of a skirt?

'No, no,' he is saying impatiently. 'Nothing to worry about. Just her age and so on. Look, I'll have a word with the hospital . . .'

'And Mo?' asks Emmy anxiously. 'She's getting so absent-minded and . . . odd.'

'She's not as young as she was,' he says comfortingly. 'Try not to worry. How old is she now? Seventy-five? She misses Pamela, of course. Look, I'll be in touch but I can't come quite as often as I'd like. You know how it is . . .'

'Oh, of course,' says Emmy at once. 'You're so good to us. I hope we don't . . . Is your wife . . . ?'

'It's just these bloody rumours,' he says. 'It's been quieter lately but I don't want it starting up again. She's still very jealous of Liv.'

'You know we never did anything that weekend,' says Emmy. 'Just met a couple of boys we'd known. Quite by chance, not arranged. Nothing happened. I wish I knew who saw us. Liv never really got over it, you know.'

'Don't tell me,' he says, angrily. 'Can't you see it's too late? Both our lives ruined.'

'Have you any idea,' asks Emmy, suddenly brave, 'who sent you that anonymous letter?'

'No,' he says bitterly, 'but I wish I'd ignored the bloody thing and thrown it in the fire!'

*       *       *

Alice returns home and goes away to university, her private knowledge stored and waiting for the right moment to be used. Shortly afterwards, Liv has a hysterectomy and goes home to convalesce. Emmy is rushed off her feet coping with her sister and her mother. Mo's absent-mindedness is really quite frightening. She leaves the kettle boiling itself dry on the hotplate and gets up in the middle of the night, thinking that it's morning. Sometimes she doesn't quite know who Emmy is and spends an entire day calling Livy 'Pamela'.

Livy, however, recovers quickly and, as autumn comes round again, spends hours sitting in the summerhouse knitting, whilst keeping an eye on Mo who dozes in a chair beside her.

'It would be lovely,' she tells Em, who appears with the tea tray, 'if it weren't for that bloody road.'

'It doesn't bother me any more,' says Em, putting the tray on the picnic table. 'I just imagine it's the sea breaking on the beach.'

'I can *see* the *cars*,' protests Liv.

'We really ought to move the summerhouse,' says Em, touching Mo gently on the knee. 'Cup of tea, Mo?'

'Oh, darling.' Mo rouses herself and looks about. 'How nice. Yes. But where is Fa? We mustn't start without Fa.'

Livy and Em exchange glances. 'Fa's not here, Mo, remember? He's gone away.'

She frowns, distressed, and Livy hastens to change the subject. 'Shall we move the summerhouse, Mo? What do you think? Where would be the best place for it?'

The girls discuss the summerhouse whilst Mo receives and sips at her tea. She drifts off for a bit and then sits up again, looking more alert.

'Fa always said,' she says, 'that he'd wished he'd built the summerhouse in the yard over the old well. It's more sheltered and looks south west.' She yawns. 'I hope you've left one in the pot for Pamela,' she says, passing her cup to Liv – and sleeps again.

She has spilled tea down her jersey which she is wearing inside out and her shoes do not match. Emmy sighs and shakes her head.

'She's OK,' says Liv, comfortingly. 'She's great, really. D'you know I hardly ever remember that she's not my mum?'

Emmy smiles reminiscently. 'Goodness, we led them a dance, didn't we?'

'We were little monsters.' Livy grimaces guiltily. 'I was so jealous of you to begin with. I was terrified that Fa might love you more than me.'

'I was the same,' sighs Em. 'And we took it out on them. All those toys . . .'

'And the trips to the seaside. And then when Rosie came . . .'

They both fall silent. They are remembering the day of Grandmother's funeral; an early day in September. Emmy can feel the berry between her fingers: the soft slightly squashy substance carefully wrapped within her handkerchief. Liv can feel the hot sun through her Aertex shirt and she sees the image of Boswell lying in the sun.

'Do you remember . . . ?' she begins slowly.

'Yes,' says Em quickly.

They stare at each other. Each longs to question the other; both are frightened at the thought. Mo wakes up suddenly and looks at them sternly.

'I think that you should both know,' she says, 'that your father is having an affair with Jessie Matthews.'

When Alice comes home from university for Easter she is already experimenting seriously with drugs. Being Roop's daughter, with a miser's love of money, she is playing with the idea of pushing drugs to the weak and vulnerable.

Meanwhile, she has to pay for her own habit. She has been thinking things over carefully and remembering and considering what she has heard.

'Did you know,' she asks Rosie one morning in the holidays, 'that Livy had an abortion once?'

Rosie stares at her in amazement. 'Are you serious?'

'Sure.' Alice yawns and fidgets a little. 'I heard Emmy and the doctor talking about it.'

Rosie's nostrils flare a little; she has smelled blood.

'What did they say?' she asks.

'What's it worth?' counters Alice.

They look at each other; like recognising like. Rosie remembers the jibes about Weight Watchers and the insults to Roop.

'It depends,' she says coolly, 'on the importance of what you heard.'

'I heard all sorts of things,' says Alice idly. 'Things about abortions and rumours upsetting the doc's wife. And a love affair from the past and a nasty sneaking anonymous letter.'

She stares at Rosie, smiling a little, and Rosie realises that Alice knows the truth. She has put two and two together and come to a startlingly lucrative conclusion.

'Why?' Alice asks curiously. 'Why did you do it?'

'Mind your own business,' says Rosie, knowing that it would be pointless to deny it.

'Imagine how upset Emmy and Liv would be if they knew,' says Alice thoughtfully. 'Not to mention the doctor. Grandmother might be pretty cross, too. Perhaps she'd cut you out of her will.'

'She's too potty to be taken seriously,' snaps Rosie – but she looks worried.

'Shall we try it?' smiles Alice. 'Isn't it the doc who says whether or not Grandmother is in her right mind?'

'How much do you want?' asks Rosie grimly.

Alice tells her and Rosie swallows. 'But you get the whole conversation for that, too,' comforts Alice. 'I won't charge you extra. You could get quite a lot of fun out of it, I promise you.'

'Tell me,' says Rosie, 'and I'll think about the money.'

'Oh, you'll pay,' says Alice. 'I have a strong feeling the doc would be on Livy and Em's side when it comes to how sound Grandmother's mind is.'

When Rosie arrives for a visit, Mo is having one of her lucid spells and Rosie discounts the idea of having Mo committed. She is obviously frail and forgetful, however, and Rosie sounds out the girls so as to assess the situation.

'Isn't it time she went into a home?' she asks, seeing anew just how desirable the property is and remembering the number of unexpected expenses she has had to meet recently.

'She's *in* a home,' says Emmy. 'Hers. Where she ought to be.'

'I'm only thinking of you,' says Rosie. 'If Mo was being looked after, you could sell up and buy yourselves a nice little flat.'

'We don't want a nice little flat,' says Emmy. 'This is our home. We like it here.'

Rosie raises her eyebrows. 'Do you like all the work that goes with it? All these rooms to clean? Carrying logs in? All that gardening?'

'Yes, we do like it,' says Liv, who is feeling better than she has for years. 'We are, however, touched by your concern for us.'

Rosie looks at her consideringly. 'You're looking good,' she says. 'Lots of bedside manner from the doctor? Is that what's put the colour in your cheeks?'

'It might be,' says Liv. 'I feel great. You, on the other hand, are not wearing well. Are you sure that it's wise to dye your hair? So ageing, don't you think? Even when you were little you were never *that* blonde. And remember that, when you've got a tummy, looser clothes make you look thinner.'

'Perhaps you shouldn't have said that,' says Em, when Rosie has stalked out.

'Why not?' asks Liv. 'Sarky bitch. All that about a bedside manner.'

'I know,' said Em. 'I don't blame you. It's just . . . I had a queer feeling of danger.'

'Don't be daft,' says Liv. 'What on earth could Rosie do to hurt us?'

# 10

Rosie does not act at once. She waits for the right psychological moment; the moment when she will be able to do the maximum amount of damage. She spends hours planning how she will deal the blow. She is temporarily distracted by Alice being sent down from university. She has been associating with some students now accused of pushing drugs. Nothing, it appears, can actually be proved in Alice's case, and, while letters are flying to and fro, she suddenly disappears. Just before she goes, she blackmails another large sum from Rosie so that when they have a postcard from her, postmarked Amsterdam and telling them that she intends to travel for a while, Rosie and Roop are relieved that the matter is out of their hands.

Rosie dismisses her daughter from her mind and goes back to plotting; Roop approaches a friend who is a property developer and secret negotiations begin. Rosie drives down to keep an eye on the situation but, fortunately, Mo is still having one of her lucid moments and Rosie knows that she must bide her time. It is clear that Emmy's capital is being eroded and the house is beginning to look shabby. Livy is no longer able to claim a disability allowance and is trying to find some kind of work and Emmy advertises for typing to be done at home.

'The trouble is,' says Rosie, her eyes on the peeling

paintwork on the window frames and the damp in the breakfast room, 'that you're a bit out of date, aren't you? Everyone's computer-literate these days. They have their own word processors and lap-tops.'

Since no one has answered Emmy's advertisement, she cannot argue; anyway, she knows Rosie is right.

Livy has applied for one or two jobs but is not even called for an interview.

'Of course,' says Rosie, noting the sparsely filled shelves in the larder and the worn patches in the rugs, 'you're getting a bit old, aren't you? Fifty-five, is it? You'll be getting the old age pension soon, won't you? Nobody's likely to offer you a job at your age.'

Rosie is underlining Livy's own fears, although Livy won't admit as much. The girls wear their best clothes whilst Rosie is with them, lest she comments on the patches and darns which decorate their everyday attire. Mo, though lucid, spends a great deal of time dozing in the sun. Rosie watches sharply, hoping that a charge of underfeeding or neglecting her can be brought, but Mo is treated with every consideration and, though there are few luxuries, Rosie eats well. She takes care to eat as much as she can and is delighted when she sees Emmy driving off to the village to buy in more stocks of food. She wonders if she can extend her stay so as to be as heavy a burden upon them as possible but is obliged to return to London to fulfil her social commitments.

'Why should we have to feed her?' fumes Livy. 'Why shouldn't she pay her share?'

'No reason,' admits Emmy, 'except that I don't want her knowing how we're placed. I don't want her getting Mo away on some pretext or other.'

'What difference does it make to her?' asks Liv. 'She's not taking any of the responsibility. And it would be Rosie and Roop who would have to fork out. *We* couldn't afford it.'

'I think,' says Emmy slowly, 'I think that they would insist that the house would have to be sold to meet the costs of the nursing home.'

Liv stares at her, frowning. 'But where would *we* live?'

'I don't think Rosie and Roop would worry too much about that,' answers Em.

They stare at each other, puzzling it out.

'No,' Liv shakes her head. 'I can't see how that would benefit them. Quite the reverse. The money would all go on fees. There would be nothing left for them. It's to their advantage to keep the house intact, although all the time we're living in it they can't do much anyway.'

'Could they turn us out?' asks Em. 'When Mo dies? What's the situation then?'

'I don't think they can do that,' says Liv confidently. 'We'd have right of tenure or something. After all we own two thirds to her third.'

'That's OK then,' says Em, relieved.

Soon after Rosie leaves, Mo has a relapse into an absent-minded phase. This time she is rather worse; she is also beginning to be incontinent. The washing machine is never silent and the girls wonder how they will cope when winter comes.

'We really need a tumble dryer,' says Em anxiously.

'You must be joking,' says Liv grimly.

They fall silent as Mo enters the kitchen, humming breathily. She is wearing a long velvet skirt in which she once graced dinner tables and parties and, over it and on top of her nightie, one of Fa's tweed jackets. She weaves unsteadily towards them and they can see Pam's flask – Grandmother's flask – sticking out of the jacket pocket. Her feet are bare.

'Good morning, good morning,' she carols. 'And how are you, my darlings?'

'We're fine, Mo,' says Em, resigned. 'Got yourself up this morning, I see. Coffee?'

'Oh darling! Yes please. I have *the* most horrid taste in my mouth. I simply can't imagine what it must be. Is Pamela up yet?'

'No,' says Liv.

They have read that they should be truthful with her on these occasions and refuse to humour her. They should gently but firmly insist on the facts and help her to face reality.

'All I can say,' cries Em in despair, 'is that the person who wrote this book has never put in any real life experience.'

So – 'No,' says Liv. 'Not yet. It's early for Pamela.'

'Naughty Pammie,' says Mo, taking out her teeth and cleaning them at the sink with the nail brush. 'She's a lazy girl. Never mind. What's for brekkies?'

'Porridge,' says Liv gently, removing the brush from Mo's thin trembling old hand. 'With brown sugar and a dash of cream.'

Flakes of mud from yesterday's scrubbed baked potatoes are now adhering to Mo's teeth which she rams gaily back into her mouth.

'Porridge,' she cries. 'Delicious. My favourite. Pee first.'

She totters out, uttering little cries, and the girls look at one another, each face reflecting the other's exasperated but very deep love for Mo. Suddenly with one accord they begin to laugh. They laugh until the tears come; staggering together, holding one another up, allowing tensions and anxieties to be washed away in this burst of healing genuine mirth. When Mo reappears they try to control themselves, although chuckles still spurt from them. She stands just inside the door, watching them slyly.

'Mo's been a naughty girl,' she says winningly.

'Oh dear,' says Em, wiping her eyes. 'What now?'

Mo coyly turns and holds out the velvet, which is very wet.

'Oh shit. She didn't pull her skirt up properly,' mutters

Liv. She puts a hand on Em's shoulder. 'I'll deal with it. You start dishing out the porridge.'

As Livy hustles Mo upstairs, Emmy begins to serve up the breakfast. Even Mo's latest mishap cannot lower her spirits. The laughter, the sharing with Liv, has strengthened her and her despair has lifted. She is frightened sometimes by the depths of the depression which takes hold of her and by the rages which come from nowhere.

'Menopause,' says Liv who, since her operation, has been on HRT and feels fit and full of energy. 'Thank God I've had everything out. Why won't you give HRT a go?'

Emmy, however, is reluctant to interfere with nature. She battles on, knowing that everything passes and soon she will be her old self again. Meanwhile such moments with Livy are precious.

'It's funny,' she says, when breakfast is over and the washing is pegged out on the line. 'I feel that you're much more my sister than Rosie is.'

'You know what Fa used to say,' says Livy, busy with the preparation of a stew. '"Molly O'Grady and the Colonel's lady are sisters under their skins." Something like that. It's a quote. Kipling.'

'Rosie certainly gets under my skin,' says Em, feelingly.

'I don't think that's quite what Kipling meant when he wrote it,' muses Liv.

'Perhaps Kipling didn't have a sister like Rosie,' says Em tartly.

Rosie and Roop are now well aware of the disadvantages of Mo being put into a nursing home. They have discovered that any monies accruing from the sale of the house might be held against her expenses.

'It wouldn't last five minutes,' says Roop. 'They cost the earth, those places. And your mother would probably take a fancy to some clever nurse and leave the whole lot to her.'

'She wouldn't be allowed to,' says Rosie. 'We'd contest it.'

'And lose it all in fees to some lawyer,' says Roop. 'No, she's got to stay where she is.'

Rosie, remembering her conversation with the girls about 'homes' and 'little flats' knows a brief moment of panic but when she remembers Emmy's reaction she feels happier again.

'They'll never put Mo in a home,' she says confidently. 'I'm sure of it.'

'That's all very well at the moment,' says Roop gloomily, 'but there may come a time when they can't cope. She might become ill and require proper nursing.'

'But she'd have to go to hospital then,' argues Rosie. 'They don't charge for you to be in hospital.'

Roop is silent, brooding. He feels that it might not be quite that straightforward. His friend, the property developer, has been down to take a look at the house, incognito of course, and has come back very excited. He has had a good scout round outside and, on the pretext of selling insurance, managed to get just inside the front door for a few moments. Roop pretends that it is still by no means decided that the house should be sold just yet and the property developer makes Roop a very nice little deal on the side, so as to help Roop and Rosie to make up their minds. Roop, unbeknownst to the property developer, has already had a second opinion and decides to tweak a few tails. By the time he has finished there is a very advantageous offer on the table for Roop and Rosie.

They decide to pay another visit to see how things are with Mo. Roop takes a few measurements and checks on one or two things which cannot be ascertained by surveying the place from the outside or a brief five minutes just inside the hall. While they are there, Mo has a little fall and the doctor is summoned. Fortunately nothing is broken and Mo recovers quite rapidly, nevertheless Livy and Em increase their vigilance. Mo doesn't recognise Rosie and takes against Roop.

'That man is here again,' she says in a piercing whisper to Liv, staring at Roop as he helps himself to cake at teatime. 'Why does he come? Who is he?'

'It's Roop, Mo,' says Liv, who is delighted to see Roop thus embarrassed. 'You remember old Roop! Pigling Bland you used to call him. Don't you remember? You used to say, "trust Pigling Bland to eat all the cakes again," and we'd all laugh. After he'd gone home, of course. Surely you remember?'

'He's eating all the cakes now,' announces Mo loudly, glaring at Roop.

'Naturally,' says Liv, shrugging. 'Old habits die hard.'

'And who is that woman he's brought with him?' asks Mo, whispering again.

'That's Rosie, Mo. Your daughter? Rosie? The Little Princess? Although she looks rather more like an old queen these days. Surely you remember Rosie?'

'No,' says Mo querulously. 'I don't want them here eating all my cakes.'

Liv laughs at Rosie's venomous expression and Roop's humiliation. 'I'm not surprised you don't recognise them, Mo. They come so seldom. Never mind. Look! Pigling Bland has left a cake for you after all.'

'They're probably trying to turn her against us,' says Rosie furiously as they drive home. 'Daft old bat.'

'I can honestly say that I dislike your sisters more each time I see them,' rages Roop. 'Especially Livy.'

'They're my *step*-sisters,' snaps Rosie, 'and they're as bad as each other.'

'Of course if they didn't have that wretched doctor dancing attendance she'd have probably been dead long ago,' says Roop viciously, still rankling at the 'Pigling Bland' jibe. 'They're on the telephone to him for every little problem. Or he's up there clucking round like an old mother hen. She'll never die at this rate.'

Rosie falls silent, an idea forming in her busy brain. She sees that the time has come to use the knowledge passed on by Alice and, in using it, she can kill two birds with one stone. She smiles a little at the apt phrase. Roop catches the smile out of the corner of his eye.

'What's funny?' he asks resentfully, changing gear and joining the motorway at speed. Is she, too, enjoying the joke at his expense?

'Don't worry,' she says, patting his knee. She knows exactly what he is thinking. 'Liv's going to regret making those remarks. She made a very expensive joke this afternoon. It's really going to cost her.'

'How d'you mean?' Roop is all agog. 'What are you talking about?'

'Never mind.' She squeezes his knee and then folds her hands in her lap, planning. 'Trust me.'

Roop, glancing sideways, feels comforted. He has every confidence in Rosie, knowing that she will never allow such a huge prize to slip from her grasping little fingers. He relaxes, concentrating on his driving, whilst, beside him, Rosie works out the details of her campaign.

# 11

Mo's relapse has given the doctor a chance to spend more time with Liv. They enjoy quiet moments together in the warm autumnal sunshine and Emmy leaves them in peace to make the most of their passionless Indian Summer.

'I expect that it wouldn't have worked,' says Liv, trying to be cheerful, as they walk across the lawns. 'I'd have driven you mad.'

'I don't think so,' he says, drawing her arm within his own. 'I'm so glad that we've had these times together.'

'So am I,' she admits – and leans against him for a brief happy moment.

It is as if they are young again but, once he is gone and she has hurried away to her room to hold on to her happiness a little longer, she sees herself in her glass and her heart sinks. Is this what *he* sees? The thin lined face? The grey hair? She looks at herself in despair and, sitting down on the edge of her bed, she stares out of the window at the gold and russet of the beeches and beyond them to the distant hills. She thinks of their young love blossoming before the anonymous letter blasted it and destroyed it; she thinks of the wasted, exhausting years, of Bill's grumbling, of sex without tenderness. Lastly she thinks about the child – and the richly tinted leaves blur with the hazy blue hills.

Emmy, who knows the pattern now, times her arrival perfectly.

'Liv.' She knocks lightly at the door. 'Could you come? Mo's asking for you – I've burnt the cakes – the washing machine's not working.'

It doesn't matter what it is as long as it pulls Liv back from the brink of despair and gets her into action. Liv comes out, biting her lips, face composed and they go downstairs together. By the time the doctor comes again, she has forgotten everything but the pleasure of his company and the comfort of his affection. Mo likes him, too. She doesn't always recognise him as her doctor but she instinctively trusts him and responds to him. He is almost the only visitor they have. Mo's old friends have been lost during the years that Pamela and Mo lived together and the remaining locals – many of the villagers are in-comers – are too wary to strike up friendships.

Emmy and Liv are too busy to notice the lack of society but the doctor's visit is a treat and they cherish him and make much of him. She of the sharp nose and glinty eyes notices that, once again, he is home a little later and is called out a little more often. She watches him, questioning him when he arrives back, searching for any incriminating evidence. Once she finds a yellow rose in his overcoat pocket.

'Where did you get this?' she asks, pouncing.

He stares at it, frowning. He remembers that Livy picked it as they walked arm-in-arm together, leaning to pluck it from the bush and saying, 'It's the last rose of summer. I might as well pick it before the frost gets it.'

As he climbed into his car, she gave it to him.

'It's a bit withered,' she says, smiling, 'and brown round the edges. Like us really. Never mind . . .' she tucks it into the buttonhole on his lapel and waves him off, still smiling.

He has had the sense to take it out of his buttonhole but cannot bear to throw it away and so has tucked it in his pocket, planning to press it into one of his own books.

'I picked it,' he says slowly. 'It was growing on a wall . . . Why are you looking in my pockets?'

'Why put it in your pocket?' she counters. 'Look. It's been crushed.' Slowly – watching him – she pulls off the petals one by one and lets them fall lightly to the floor. 'Ruined,' she says. 'Finished. Dead. What a pity, isn't it?'

He turns away from her, a mist before his eyes that makes him stumble a little. When he has shut himself into his study she stamps upon the petals and searches his briefcase thoroughly. She hears that Mo is failing and knows that his visits are perfectly legitimate but she guesses how they are stretched to include chats and tea – and love and tender words? – and she fumes helplessly.

When the telephone call comes she is shocked into silence. The voice whispers gently in her ear whilst she clutches the receiver . . .

'Ask him,' whispers the voice, 'ask him about the abortion that Livy Faringdon had. Ask him who the father was and why she had to have an abortion. She was married, wasn't she? Why should she have an abortion? Perhaps her legitimate husband was unable to father a child? Perhaps they were not sharing a bed at that time? Why was it all hushed up? Ask him . . .'

There is a silence. The glinty eyes are glintier than ever; the nose pointier . . .

'But be careful,' rustles the voice. 'You don't want him struck off, do you? That won't do you any good. Be sensible. A bit of gentle blackmail? Early retirement? Must be worrying for you having her so close. Move right away somewhere. Haven't you got a daughter in York? Must be a long drive to York . . .'

Insistently the thoughts are transplanted into her mind and, when the caller clicks off suddenly, she realises that she should have made some effort to find out who it was. She doesn't even know whether the voice was male or female; she is too shocked to really care. Something tells her that the information is reliable. At first she is filled with fury; her jealousy is violent. Presently she calms down a little, steadying herself and plotting her revenge. She mulls this over very carefully, her spirits rising. She has longed to move nearer to her daughter and this gives her the opportunity for which she has been waiting. Of course, she must not let him think that she won't split on him if necessary, this is her weapon, but she must wield it carefully. He must be spurred and driven by it; not cudgelled to death.

She chooses her moment carefully, waiting for an evening when he is tired and dispirited. Her words dart across the supper table like tiny poisoned arrows.

'This affair with Livy, then,' she says, serving up the shepherd's pie. 'So when was it? God, you were careful, weren't you? I never suspected a thing.'

'Affair?' He gapes at her, but his guilt – he loves Livy more than he loves his wife – makes him clumsy. 'I haven't. We don't . . .'

'I'm not talking about now,' she says, eyes glinting. 'I'm talking about when you made her pregnant. When she had the abortion.'

He stares at her dumbfounded. How on earth can she possibly know about the abortion?

'How . . . How . . . ?' he stammers. Too late, he pulls his addled wits together. 'What abortion? What on earth are you talking about?'

She leans forward, rapping the table. 'I'm talking about Livy Faringdon's abortion.' She snorts impatiently. 'Oh, I don't know what her married name is. Who cares? But why should a respectable married woman have an abortion unless the child is not her husband's?'

'The child was certainly not mine,' he cries – and falls into the trap.

'So you admit there was a child and that she got rid of it?' she asks softly, the pointy nose quivering.

'No. No I don't,' he says desperately. 'I admit nothing. I know nothing.'

She smiles. 'Liar,' she says pleasantly. 'You've been carrying on with her all the time, haven't you?'

'No!' he shouts. 'I've told you that there's nothing between us. It's your imagination. I feel nothing for her.' He shuts his eyes for a moment, asking Liv's forgiveness for such a betrayal, yet knowing that he is trying to save her from this glinty-eyed, sharp-nosed woman. 'Nothing,' he says, quietly but firmly.

'In that case you won't care if you don't see her again,' says she sweetly, shiny with triumph. 'You know, you're looking tired. Old. I think that you should take early retirement. You know how much I'd like to move to York to be near Jen.'

He watches her, waiting. She nods at him.

'You must choose, of course. But it would be a pity if the story of the abortion leaked out. There will be plenty of people ready to believe it. Heavens!' She laughs lightly. 'They may even believe that you even got rid of the baby for her. Would the practice keep you on with that sort of rumour going about? Would your life be worth it anyway? Or hers?'

'This is madness,' he whispers. 'You can't believe that she ... that I ... Oh, God. Who on earth told you this rubbish?'

'Oh, it's not rubbish,' she says, smiling. 'I can see it's not rubbish. Tell you what? Why don't I phone Livy and ask *her* about it?'

'No!' he shouts, as she stands up and reaches for the wall telephone. 'No ...'

He strikes away her outstretched hand and then sinks down, dropping his head in his hands.

'So.' She leans over him, rejoicing yet hating him. 'It's York, is it?'

'Yes,' he says dully. 'It's York.'

'What could I do?' he asks Livy. 'She knew. Who could have told her? She says that someone telephoned her. A well-wisher.'

'Who told *you*?' asks Livy, lips stiff. 'Was it Emmy?'

'No,' he says quickly. 'Not Em. I knew the moment I examined you. There were . . . signs. And I knew you had no children, you see. I guessed and then I made Em tell me the truth. She didn't want to. It doesn't *matter*, Liv. Nothing matters except that I have to go.'

'Yes,' she says. 'You have to go.'

She stares away from him proudly and he watches her, his eyes full of tears.

'If I stayed,' he says gently, 'she would see that all our lives are ruined. The rumours would be intolerable. You would be gossiped about. There would be sniggers and probably even rejection. At the shop and so on. People can be funny about things like this. You and Em and Mo are too vulnerable. Please try to understand. I am trying to protect you.'

'Yes,' she says dully. 'Yes, I know.'

'What else can I do?' he cries, trying to penetrate the stony distance between them. 'Shall I leave her? Shall we go away somewhere together?'

For a moment Liv is tempted to cry, 'Yes!' To fling herself at him and grab what little love there might be left to them. Suddenly she remembers the thin lined face and the grey hair, the self that confronts her in the glass, and she grasps at her dignity. They are too old for such notions.

'No,' she says gently. 'Think of the fuss. The divorce and so on. You have children and grandchildren. It is too late for

us. I must stay with Emmy and Mo. They need me here.' She
shakes her head, her eyes filling with tears. 'However shall
we manage without you?'

'I don't know.' He is thinking about Mo. The timing
couldn't be worse. He cudgels his brains again. '*Who* could
have told her? *Who*? Could Bill have decided to exact some
kind of revenge for your walking out on him?'

'But why?' asks Liv helplessly. 'Why now? That was
years ago.'

'But who else is there?' he asks.

They fall silent. In the shadows of the rhododendrons
he pulls her into his arms and they kiss – oh! how desperately they cling to each other – for the first time for
thirty-five years.

'We have a few weeks left,' he says. 'I've promised to wait
until they find a locum. Even *she* can't argue with that. I
wonder if I dare call her bluff. Would she dare to spread
such a rumour? She'd suffer as much as we would.'

'Either way,' says Livy, holding him tightly, 'she can make
your life hell. At least in York you'll have your daughter. You
love your daughter.'

'Yes,' he says miserably. 'I love you, too, Liv.'

They kiss again but they know that it is too late for them.
Once again their happiness has been destroyed anony-
mously. A few weeks later he is gone.

'It's too cruel,' says Emmy. 'I can't believe that this can
happen to you a second time. Who told her? Who knew?'

Liv is too tired and too unhappy to continue with speculation. She feels ill and weak.

'Bill knew,' she says flatly. 'And you knew. No one else.'

'There must be someone else,' reasons Em. 'Why on earth
should Bill bother to interfere in your life at this late date?
He's been shacked up with that woman ever since you
left him.'

'Well then,' says Liv wearily, 'that just leaves you.'

Em stares at her in amazement. 'I hope you're not suggesting that *I* did it.'

Liv shrugs. For a very black moment, she wonders if Em just might have done it during one of her fits of depression. Perhaps she was jealous . . . ? Em is watching her, shocked and hurt, and there is a current of distrust suddenly blowing between them.

'Look, I'm exhausted,' says Liv evasively. 'Let's not get things out of proportion. I'm not suggesting anything . . .' but the seed is sown.

# 12

When Rosie arrives to see the results of her handiwork, she is delighted to see a coolness between Emmy and Liv. It has already occurred to her that Liv might suspect Em – even if only for lack of other suspects – but she quickly guesses that there might be other reasons which she can utilise to her own advantage. As she sits at the kitchen table while Liv peels potatoes she comments quietly on Emmy's mood swings.

'At times I wonder,' she says, 'if she's quite right in the head.' She pauses, waiting for the put-down she would certainly have received only a few weeks earlier. She notes the silence and moves on smoothly. 'It's not all the time, of course. Just odd moments. Like she's another person. Frightening really. She might do anything.'

She lets this sink in and sips her coffee reflectively.

'It's just the menopause,' growls Livy at last. 'Nothing to worry about.'

'Oh, I'm sure you're right,' agrees Rosie. 'Still, it must be difficult for you. Never know where you are from one minute to the next, I should think.'

'It's not that bad,' says Livy shortly. 'I cope.'

'I know you do,' says Rosie admiringly. 'Rather you than me. I can imagine you two going on together right to the end.' She laughs affectionately. 'Unless old Em does something desperate in a mad moment.'

• Willa Marsh

Livy is silent. Her suspicion has grown a little in the last few weeks and Rosie's words are encouraging it. *Could* Emmy have done such a thing, even in her deepest depression?

'Have you ever noticed,' asks Rosie, cosily confidential, 'that Em's jealous of you?' She notices the stiffening of Liv's spine. 'Even when I was very small I noticed it. Especially when you got engaged first.'

'How could you have noticed?' asks Liv, after a small but very telling pause. 'You were a child.'

'Mmm.' Rosie nods. 'But children notice everything. I remember she said one or two things to Mo and Mo slapped her down. And then I remember something about her persuading you to go away for a weekend and afterwards your engagement was broken off. I always wondered why. And then she rushed you off to London, remember? Fa was cross because he had to sell your flat.'

Liv continues to peel potatoes but her brain is reeling. Could the whole thing have been a plot on Em's part? Desperately she tries to remember back to that time . . .

'Machine's finished,' says Rosie brightly. 'I'll hang out the washing, shall I?'

'Thanks,' says Liv mechanically. 'If you could.'

'No trouble,' sings out Rosie, unloading the wet clothes into the laundry basket. 'Goodness, I don't envy you all this work, especially now old Betty's ill and you can't get help. I was looking at the estate agents in the town yesterday. Prices are going up again round here, aren't they? There was a lovely little house down by the river. Very quiet and private. Still, I know how you feel about hanging on here . . .'

'I couldn't leave Emmy and Mo,' says Liv – but the usual vehemence is missing.

'Oh, I was thinking of after Mo . . . you know. But I'm sure you and Em will stick together . . .'

She goes out into the blowy morning and Liv stands,

hands stilled, staring out of the window. At this moment, the idea of a quiet little cottage is very appealing. It would be very pleasant to be alone; no Emmy; no Mo . . .

'After all,' Rosie is back to fetch the pegs, 'Mo's not your mother is she? And Emmy isn't your sister. Not like you and me sharing a father. There's no blood relation at all . . .'

The words hang in the air after she has gone. Presently Liv goes upstairs and sits on her bed, thinking.

'Have you noticed,' asks Rosie, when Liv has taken Mo out for a little drive in the car and she and Emmy are washing up after lunch, 'that Liv is acting a bit strangely lately?'

Hurt by Liv's suspicion and coolness, Emmy does not immediately respond with a defensive retort. Rosie smiles to herself.

'I just wondered,' she says, 'if it might be to do with the hysterectomy?'

'How do you mean?' asks Emmy cautiously, scrubbing at a dish.

Rosie notices that Emmy does not refute her suggestion out of hand as once would have been the case. 'I've read that operations can bring on peculiar reactions,' she says, 'and she's at a difficult age, of course . . .'

'So am I,' says Em pointedly.

'Oh, I know,' says Rosie quickly. 'But you're coping very well with it. I don't trust this HRT stuff Liv's on. Messing about with nature. And, of course Liv's always been jealous of you, hasn't she?'

'Whatever do you mean?' Emmy turns to look at her, frowningly. 'We were always treated exactly the same.'

'Oh, I know,' says Rosie, laughing placatingly. 'I know *that*. But Mo was your real mother and Fa adored you and I think Liv could never *quite* get over that. And then, Martin was such a nice chap and you were so comfortable and Liv was so miserable with that ghastly Bill. I feel that this jealousy is just underneath all the time, undermining her affection for you. Sad really, especially when you get on so well most of the time.'

'We're very close,' says Em – but there is a lack of conviction in her voice.

'Oh, I know you are,' says Rosie quickly. 'It's great. Especially as you're not real sisters.'

'What do you mean?' asks Emmy surprised.

'Well, you and Liv aren't sisters, are you? There's no blood relation. Not like between you and me, sharing a mother.'

Emmy pulls out the plug and watches the water swooshing away. Rosie's words unsettle her and she feels a strange anxiety.

'It's when the chips are down you notice it,' Rosie is saying as she puts away the plates. 'Blood's thicker than water. No doubt about that.'

During Rosie's stay there is no requirement to call the doctor out to Mo but Rosie feels sure that, had he still been about, he would have turned up on some pretext or other. She decides to keep silent on the subject but drops in at the health centre for an update. She remembers that she was at school with one of the administrators who was – and still is – a great gossip and she invites her out to lunch. She is only too ready to tell Rosie the latest scandal and how they are all upset by their favourite doctor's sudden departure for York. The story is that his daughter is the reason for his decision to retire a little early and there is speculation about her health. Perhaps another baby – rather late after the others – is on the way? Rosie can't resist stirring the waters and disturbing a little mud.

'Do you remember that he was engaged to my sister?' she asks idly. 'She's missing him terribly. So's my mother, of course, but Livy . . .' Rosie shakes her head as if she cannot find words capable of expressing Livy's grief.

The friend stares at her, round-eyed. The health centre is in the town and so none of the staff has been aware of the doctor's regular calls to the house on the hill.

'They were childhood sweethearts,' says Rosie sadly, 'and then things went wrong for them. Liv moved away but when she came back she was *so* pleased to see him. They're such good friends . . . Goodness, she's going to miss him. He was always dropping in . . . to check on my mother. Liv's taken it really hard. So has my mother, of course.'

'Of course,' says the friend – but her eyes are avid. She can hardly wait to get back and discuss it with her colleagues.

Rosie, who has chosen her *confidante* carefully, smiles and waves as they part after lunch.

'So how were they?' asks Roop when she gets back home.

'OK.' She smiles a satisfied smile. 'Everything's under control.'

'I wish you'd tell me what you've been up to,' he grumbles. He looks a little sulky. Rosie has played this one very close to her chest.

'Don't grump,' she chides, bending to kiss him on his sparsely covered head. 'You know you can trust me.'

'But *you* can't trust *me* by the sound of it,' he says, refusing to be wheedled out of his sulks. He wants to know every little detail so that he can gloat.

'I already explained it to you,' she says tenderly, sitting on the arm of his chair. 'You're such a kindly guileless old thing that I can't risk Livy or Em trapping you. You know how devious they are?'

Roop, who is as kindly and guileless as the butcher bird, is certainly gullible when it comes to flattery. Nothing is too gross.

'You're probably right,' he admits, sighing heavily.

'I know I am,' she says, snuggling closer. She has no

intention of ever admitting her part in her sisters' smashed love affairs; not even to Roop.

The new doctor is a middle-aged woman. She is bright and cheerful, with a head of youthfully bubbly curls and a determined smile. Mo stares at her unwinkingly, huddled in her bed. She has missed the doctor but is too vague now to understand the real situation.

'Who's this woman?' she asks Em.

Emmy smiles quickly at the doctor – who smiles back.

'Don't mind me, dear,' she says briskly. 'I quite understand how it is.'

'I do hope so,' murmurs Em. 'Mo, this is the doctor.'

'No, it isn't,' says Mo instantly. 'I know the doctor. He's a man. She's not the doctor. She's tricking us.' She narrows her eyes, cudgelling her recalcitrant brain. 'I used to know who she is . . .' she says slowly.

'Please Mo,' says Emmy desperately. 'She *is* the doctor.'

'No,' shouts Mo. 'No. I know who she is. She's Jessie Matthews. It's a trick. She's come to see Fa . . . Oooohhh,' Mo begins to moan. 'How could he? Under our very roof. Ooohh . . .'

Emmy hustles the doctor out quickly whilst Livy deals with Mo. The doctor's smile is less determined and her eyes are watchful.

'What's all this about Jessie Matthews?' she asks.

'Nothing,' says Emmy, trying to laugh it off. 'It's something that's happened since my father died. Take no notice. I'm so sorry.'

She heads her off on to the more general topic of Mo's health and, when she's gone, goes back to the bedroom. Liv is sitting on the bed watching Mo who, having had a few sips from her flask, is calmer now. Liv and Emmy look at one another. For some reason, this little scene has had the effect of pushing back their distrust and, for the first time for weeks, they feel closer, more as they did before the anonymous telephone call. Mo, lying back on her pillows, begins to hum.

'Over my shoulder goes *one* care . . .' She giggles a little.

'For God's sake,' says Liv feelingly, 'don't let that woman see Mo's flask.'

Emmy begins to chuckle. 'Did you see her face?' she asks. 'Jessie Matthews. Honestly!'

'To be fair,' says Liv, 'she *does* have a look of her. It's those curls . . .' She, too, begins to chuckle. 'Good old Mo.'

'Over my shoulder go *two* cares,' hums Mo with a little tossing motion. She opens her eyes and looks at them slyly. 'Has Jessie gone?' she asks. 'Naughty, naughty Fa . . .'

She dozes and the girls sigh.

'Poor old Fa,' says Emmy. 'Nobody could have been a more devoted and faithful husband. I wonder where she got this thing about Jessie Matthews?'

'People get funny ideas,' says Liv . . . and falls silent. Has she had funny ideas about Emmy? As she looks at her she wonders how she could have imagined that Em might betray her. She remembers how Em cared for her when she was ill and how much they've shared; the burdens and the laughter. Nevertheless, Rosie's words seem to cling under her skin like tiny burs. Was Emmy jealous when she, Liv, got engaged? Did she engineer the weekend? Did it all come back in a kind of menopausal fit which was the cause of Em making the telephone call? Looking at Em, as she stands by Mo's bed, it seems impossible; but if not Emmy, then who . . . ?

Em stares back at her, wondering if Liv is really jealous of her. Did she grudge her Fa's love and Martin's security? Has her operation and the HRT given her such strange fancies that she can seriously imagine that she, Emmy, could deliberately destroy her happiness?

'Honestly, Liv,' she says gently, 'honestly, it wasn't me.'

Before Liv can answer, Mo jolts awake, drops her flask and lets out a loud yell as she scrabbles in amongst the bedclothes.

'Oh, darlings,' she says pathetically, clutching the flask to her bony chest. 'Such a horrid dream. I dreamed that Jessie Matthews came in here and took away Pammie's flask. No one must ever have Pammie's flask. I'm keeping it for her.'

The flask is placed safely on the bedside table and Mo is tucked up for an afternoon rest. The moment of intimacy has passed but the girls go downstairs with a new – or rather, the old – friendship beginning to flow back between them.

# 13

It is unfortunate for Rosie and Roop that Alice arrives home unexpectedly and prevents Rosie from visiting the girls again. Alice is not well – a chest infection – and Rosie is obliged to look after her, thereby losing the opportunity to stir up more discontent between Livy and Em. Alice is thin and, despite a tan, looks unhealthy. She recovers quite quickly, however, and begins to put the pressure on Rosie.

'What happened about that doctor?' she asks one afternoon. 'Did you put my information to good use?'

'It's none of your business,' replies Rosie, her heart sinking.

Alice laughs. 'Come off it,' she says good-humouredly. 'So what did you do? Write another anonymous letter?'

'Shush!' says Rosie sharply. Roop might walk in at any moment. 'This is between you and me.'

'Is it?' asks Alice, interestedly. 'Oh. You should have said so before.'

'Why?' Rosie looks at her anxiously. 'Have you said anything to your father? Or anyone . . . ?'

'No.' Alice smiles at her mother's fear. 'No. I haven't. Not yet. It just puts the price up, that's all.'

'Forget it,' bluffs Rosie. 'You get no more out of me.'

Alice yawns contemptuously. 'Why don't you want Dad to know?' she asks curiously. 'Think he'd be shocked?'

Rosie doesn't quite know why except that she fears that it might give Roop some kind of hold over her. They are both unscrupulous but, as far as Roop knows, their cheating and lying have been done in tandem for the benefit of both and neither one can accuse the other. Rosie lives by the motto 'if you're not one up, you're one down' and she has no intention of giving Roop any weapons to use. Alice is watching her closely.

'What a wonderful relationship you two have,' she observes. 'Such trust. So. I shall be needing some money for my fare.'

'Are you going soon?' asks Rosie eagerly – and Alice bursts out laughing.

'Control yourself, Mother dear,' she says. 'You shall have the benefit of my company a little longer. But yes, soon I shall be on my way again. How much is it worth to get rid of me?'

Rosie is silent. She knows that she is a fool to trust her daughter; that Alice would betray her without a thought if the price were right. Nevertheless, she also knows that if she doesn't pay up, Alice will tell Roop and the girls everything. She wonders if she could bluff her way out of it; tell them that Alice is a head case . . .

'Forget it,' says Alice. 'You haven't got a hope.'

Deep down, Rosie believes that she is right. She imagines her sisters' reaction and wonders if, even now, they might be able to influence Mo against her. The doctor has been safely removed, there could be no collusion there, but Mo still has relatively sane moments . . . Rosie flinches inwardly as she thinks of how Roop would react if she lost her share in the house.

'Got there?' asks Alice. 'Thinking sensibly? Good. Shall we do a few sums?'

Unknown to Rosie, Mo is deteriorating fast. Her lucid

moments are now few and far between and Livy and Em have to watch her all the time. Unless they lock her in or tie her down she is a continual danger to herself. Rosie's chat to her old friend at the health centre hasn't had quite the effect she hoped; the whispers and sidelong glances have merely served to draw Emmy and Liv even closer together. They are united in their care and anxiety for Mo and, as Christmas approaches, the rift between them has been healed. Emmy moves her bed into Mo's big bedroom, lest she should go wandering, and she is rarely left unaccompanied.

The rumours about Livy and the doctor percolate back to the village, who are only too ready to believe them, and the girls' reputations are damaged further after one bossy, interfering woman walks up to the house to see if she can lend a hand. There is no true charity in this offer; she merely wishes to have a good look round and, if she's lucky, add a juicy bit of meat to the dry bones of rumour. It is unfortunate that she picks a day which has been an arduous one for Livy and Em. Mo has been difficult, falling over, burning herself, wetting herself, looking for Pammie and Fa. After a late lunch, the girls get her into bed where she falls at once into a heavy sleep.

'I'm exhausted,' says Emmy, who has been up half the night with Mo. 'I could sleep for a week.'

'Go and put your feet up by the fire,' advises Liv. 'I'll wash up and then go out for a stroll round the garden. I need some fresh air.'

They part and, within minutes, Emmy is asleep by the fire in the breakfast room. They rarely use the drawing room now; it is too big to heat economically. Liv finishes the drying up, puts away the plates and wanders into the garden. Upstairs, Mo suddenly awakes. She lies for a moment, listening to the voice that has summoned her, clutching her flask. The voice seems to be further away now . . . She strains to hear it.

Shaking her head in frustration, she climbs from bed and patters to the door.

'Co-ming,' she calls on two notes. '*Cooo*-ming.'

She negotiates the stairs carefully, holding the bannister in her right hand and Pamela's flask in the left. For warmth, she wears one of Fa's old striped pyjama jackets over her winceyette nightie but the late November afternoon, though bright, is cold and she shivers as she pauses in the hall listening for the voice. As she hesitates, the harsh crank of the front door bell breaks the silence. In the breakfast room, Emmy wakes and stares muzzily about her but Mo advances down the hall and flings wide the door. On the step stands a stranger. Mo's brow wrinkles.

'Was it you who called?' she asks, disappointed. 'I thought it was Pammie. Or Fa.'

The woman, shocked by Mo's appearance, steps into the hall and looks eagerly around.

'Are you all on your own, dear?' she asks disapprovingly yet delightedly; eyes sharp, ears alert. 'Surely there's somebody here with you.'

Emmy, dragging herself back to wakefulness, appears at the door of the breakfast room just as Liv comes up the steps from the garden and into the hall.

'Darlings!' cries Mo, 'there's a person.' She sits down suddenly on the bottom step. 'I thought it was Pammie,' she says sadly. 'Or Fa.'

Emmy and Liv, exchanging horrified glances, hurry forward.

'What are you doing out of bed?' asks Emmy, helping Mo to her feet. 'Come in by the fire . . .'

'Can I help you?' asks Liv, herding the woman back to the front door and out onto the steps.

The bossy woman, though resenting the term 'person', is more than satisfied as she is headed off down the drive, giving advice as she goes. Already sentences are forming in her head . . . 'My dear, you should have seen her. Cold as death the house is and there she was, wandering about on her own in a ragged old nightie and a man's pyjama jacket. Nothing on her feet. One of her daughters was asleep by the fire, no doubt about that, and the other strolling about in the garden. And in her hand,' the voice drops, 'the old woman was carrying a *hip-flask* . . .'

'Oh, Mo,' says Emmy sadly. 'How could you? Now it'll be all over the village that we don't look after you properly.'

'Did you recognise her?' asks Liv of Emmy. 'Not a local, is she?'

'No,' says Emmy, resigned. 'She'll be a first generation country dweller, fresh from the city, who knows just how the countryside should be run and how the villagers should live.'

'Shit,' says Livy. 'She'll be on to the social services then.'

The bossy one telephones the health centre but the doctor, she of the Jessie Matthews curls, is curt with her. She knows that Emmy and Liv are very caring and sensible with Mo and are doing their best under difficult circumstances. Moreover, there is no room for Mo in the local hospital and, since her daughters are prepared to take responsibility for her, so much the better. Doctor Jessie Matthews is firm with the bossy woman – who is cross at being so summarily dismissed and adds a little more embroidery to her tale – but she drops by after surgery to check that all is well.

'And what's all this I hear,' she says gaily, curls bobbing, 'about a *flask*?'

Mo shrinks before the bright smile and the hard glittering eyes and hides the flask under the bedclothes. Emmy and Liv stand still as statues. Because the doctor's call is unexpected, they have not been able to take the precaution of emptying and rinsing out the flask or hiding it away.

'It's a keepsake,' says Liv quickly. 'It belonged to my aunt.

She and Mo were great friends. She lived here for years with her after Fa died. She refuses to be separated from it.'

'I understand,' says Doctor Jessie Matthews jovially, 'that your Grandmother and your aunt enjoyed a drink.'

'You've been listening to gossip,' says Emmy pleasantly. 'Mo's flask is empty. She keeps it with her in memory of Pamela, as a child might cuddle a teddy bear.'

Liv shoots her a quick glance. Em sounds very confident.

'May I see it?' asks Doctor Jessie Matthews playfully, advancing on the cowering Mo. 'May I see your lovely flask?'

The girls hold their breath as Mo slowly draws out her hand and passes over the flask to her inquisitor . . . who looks at it, unscrews the lid and tilts it . . . It is empty. Emmy closes her eyes in relief and Liv swallows. Doctor Jessie Matthews sniffs at it and passes it back to the waiting Mo.

'It smells of gin,' she says suspiciously.

'I'm not surprised,' says Emmy brightly. 'That's what Pamela used to keep in it.'

'I'm sure I don't have to tell you,' she says, eyes on the two girls, 'the effect that alcohol would have on your mother in her condition.'

'No,' says Livy feelingly. 'You certainly don't.'

When Liv has seen her off the premises, she comes back to find Mo wrapped up and sitting in the armchair whilst Emmy strips the sheets which smell strongly of gin.

'Clever old Mo,' says Liv admiringly, taking in the scene at a glance. 'But how did you know she'd done it.'

'I didn't know for sure but I guessed,' says Em, breathing hard as she pulls and folds and punches the bed back together. 'She had the most suspiciously bland smile on her face and I could see her hands moving stealthily under the bedclothes. But I was terrified.' She laughs with relief. 'When she tilted the flask I thought I might die.'

'That'll learn her,' says Liv cheerfully. 'You've got to be up early to catch Mo.'

'That old bat must have told her about the flask,' says Em, turning back the clean sheet. 'Nosy old besom. Come on, Mo. In you get.'

Clutching the flask, Mo climbs obediently between the sheets, humming breathily, beaming at the girls. 'Over my shoulder goes it *all*,' she sings and collapses contentedly among the pillows.

'Unless, of course,' says Liv thoughtfully, as they go downstairs together, 'it was our anonymous friend.' Emmy shoots a sharp anxious look at her but Liv shakes her head. 'No, no. That's all over. We were both a bit mad, I think. I know I was.'

'This bloody menopause,' says Emmy with relief. 'No, I think this time it was just gossip. That old bat who came nosing round must have gone haring back with the news. You must admit it looked awful. God!' she eases her aching back. 'I'd kill for a cup of tea!'

'No need for that,' says Liv easily. 'Go and light the fire and I'll get the kettle on.'

'I was wondering,' says Rosie to Roop, 'whether we ought to go down and see the girls and Mo for Christmas?'

Roop looks a bit put out. He likes to enjoy himself at Christmas and he can already hear the girls' stinging remarks. He frowns a little.

'Must we?' he asks plaintively. 'They won't get anything decent in and I shall feel guilty every time I eat a mince pie.'

'Poor darling,' purrs Rosie. She has made a flying visit and is uneasy by the obvious truce between her sisters. She is furious with herself for not making the effort to check that all was going as she planned.

'Anyway,' says Roop, who is in petulant mood, 'you said

you were going to get even with Livy. You said you'd make her pay for being so rude the last time I was there.'

'And so I have, my sweet,' says Rosie amiably. 'I have seen to it that her doctor friend is off the scene.'

'*Really?*' breathes Roop. 'You didn't tell me. However did you manage it?'

'Never you mind,' smiles Rosie teasingly. 'I've done it. I thought it might be amusing to go down and see how they're managing without him. Should be good for a few jokes, wouldn't you say?'

Roop can already hear the jests forming in his brain. 'Oh yes,' he says eagerly. 'Definitely. OK. We'll go. But we'll take some stuff ourselves. I'm not starving to death over Christmas.'

'Good idea,' says Rosie. If Livy and Em have to feel grateful it will make the festive season even more bitter for them. 'You can be Father Christmas. And they won't be able to refuse because of Mo. That'll really get up their noses.'

'You know,' says Roop thoughtfully, 'I think we might have quite a lot of fun after all.'

'Rosie and Roop want to come for Christmas,' says Emmy to Liv.

'Shit,' says Liv. 'Do we have to?'

'It might be Mo's last,' says Em. 'She's Rosie's mother, too. We can hardly say no.'

'We can't afford them,' protests Liv. 'Not with Pigling Bland eating his head off.'

'Rosie says they'll bring all the food with them.' Emmy shakes her head. 'I can't think what's come over her. It will look so churlish if we refuse.'

'If you say so,' says Liv reluctantly. 'OK. But it'll be hell.'

14 ∫

Emmy and Liv decide that they must make the best of things and see that Christmas is as good as they can make it. Em is right; it might be Mo's last. If Rosie and Roop are generous enough to bring the food then they must make efforts in other directions. They go up to the attics to find the decorations of yesteryear and buy a tall tree for the hall. They order extra logs and spend several days warming and airing the drawing room. Mo watches with interest, sipping from her flask, well wrapped in woollies and shawls.

By Christmas Eve when Rosie and Roop are due to arrive, the house is warm and festive. Emmy tests the lights on the tree and Livy and Mo clap when they glow into tiny points of multi-coloured life. The girls put their presents beneath the tinselly branches and pour themselves a drink. As they stand beside the tree their memories travel backwards to other Christmases.

'It reminds me of that year we came home together,' says Liv dreamily. 'We came in and there was the tree. And we put our presents underneath and Fa switched on the lights. He'd made one of Pamela's cocktails. And later we went to Midnight Mass. Remember?'

'Yes,' says Em tightly. 'I remember.'

Liv looks at her, puzzled. It is a moment or two before she

also remembers that it was the Christmas that Em brought her lawyer home to meet the family.

'Oh God!' she says, horrified. 'Sorry, Em. It slipped my mind. Sorry.'

'It's OK.' Emmy shrugs, surprised that it still hurts. 'Water under the bridge and all that.' She frowns and sips at her drink. 'It was just so *odd*!' she bursts out suddenly. 'He wasn't *like* that. I know it sounds wicked but for ages I hated Rosie more than I hated him. Although it wasn't her fault.'

'Wasn't it?' asks Liv slowly. A flash of light briefly illuminates these dark mysteries and she gropes after it. 'What was Rosie doing curled up with him on the sofa in the first place?'

'How d'you mean?' Em is frowning again.

Before Liv can answer there is a loud crash and a scream. Together they rush into the dining room where Mo has been attempting to top up her flask from the gin bottle which is now lying on the floor. By the time everything has been cleared up and Mo comforted, Rosie and Roop are arriving. They bustle in with boxes of goodies, a turkey, several bottles of wine.

'Hi, big Sis,' says Roop offensively, kissing Livy across the box he carries. With such bounty under her nose it is difficult to be rude; and it *is* Christmas.

Livy swallows down her natural instincts and smiles thinly.

'Bring it all through to the kitchen,' she says. 'Hello, Rosie. Good trip?'

'Look, Mo,' Emmy is saying in the drawing room. 'Here are Rosie and Roop.'

She has tucked Mo's flask well out of sight, putting her finger to her lips and making the same signs of secrecy that she makes when Doctor Jessie Matthews comes. Mo seems to understand that she must be cautious. She remembers how the precious flask was taken from her for those few terrible moments and she responds accordingly to Em's warnings when she thinks she is in danger of losing it again. She snuggles down into her cushions, the flask well hidden; she looks like an old hen settling on its nest, protecting a clutch of eggs.

'Hello, Mo.' Rosie leans over to kiss her and Mo shuts her eyes.

'Thank you for calling,' she says distinctly. 'Please close the door when you leave.'

Rosie straightens up and stares at Emmy. 'Well!' she says, laughing a touch mirthlessly. 'That's a nice welcome, I must say.'

'It's no good getting upset,' says Emmy soothingly, hiding her amusement. 'It's just one of those days. And it's late for Mo. She's usually tucked up in bed by now. She's stayed up to see you. She's eighty-one, remember, and she hasn't been well.'

Rosie swallows her indignation and shrugs. 'We've brought lots of food with us,' she says. 'And drink. We know how you all like a drink in this house.'

'True,' says Em, who has vowed that she will not let Rosie get under her skin. The thought makes her smile and she hums a line of verse. '*The Colonel's Lady and Judy O'Grady are sisters under their skins.*'

'You sound cheerful,' says Rosie, almost accusingly.

She has been taken aback by the glowing tree, the decorations and the blazing fire – not quite the picture of poverty she'd hoped for – and she sees that there is amity between Liv and Em. She knows that she should have been back to fuel and fan those flames of distrust and she is angry. She can see that there might be problems ahead, when Mo dies, if the girls are in close alliance.

'I *am* cheerful,' says Emmy. 'It's Christmas.'

'Em's made some mince pies,' says Livy, coming in with a plateful, followed closely by Roop. 'She knows how you and

119 •

Roop love them. A drink and a mince pie or two will keep
you going until dinner.'

Roop waits for some sarcastic remark but none is forth-
coming and he tucks in happily. Emmy makes delicious
little mince pies, liberally sprinkled with sugar, and he is
already on his second by the time Livy has poured the
drinks. She bites back the acid comment that rises to her
lips and hands him a glass. She has poured a small one for
Mo and Emmy puts it into her hand and crouches beside
her chair.

'Come on, Mo,' she says. 'Let's drink a toast. Happy
Christmas.'

Mo looks surprised to be offered a legitimate drink. She sits
up straighter and pats her hair, holding the glass gingerly.

'Happy Christmas,' she says obediently – but she looks
about her cautiously. 'Is Jessie Matthews coming?'

'No,' says Em.

'Is *who* coming?' asks Roop with his mouth full.

'No one,' says Liv quickly. 'It's just a joke. So. Happy
Christmas.'

Before she leaves, Rosie does her best to sow mistrust. This
time it is much more difficult and she is obliged to be far
less subtle.

'Poor Liv,' she says sympathetically on Christmas evening
when they are alone after tea. 'You must miss your doctor
friend. No, I mean it. I know we used to josh you about him
but it's really sad he's gone.'

'Who told you he's gone?' asks Liv after a moment or two.

'Emmy,' says Rosie glibly, taking a chance. 'She doesn't
seem to be too bothered – she seemed quite pleased, I
thought – but *you* must feel it a bit.'

'I get by,' says Liv – but she is thoughtful and quiet.

Rosie is anxious to make her point. 'What happened to
him?' she asks.

Liv shrugs. 'Retired. Moved away.'

'Bit sudden, wasn't it?' persists Rosie.

'Very sudden,' agrees Livy.

'How odd,' muses Rosie, her eyes on Liv's closed face.

'Mmm,' says Liv – and falls silent.

Rosie takes heart by this silence. She has reminded Liv of the suspicious circumstances surrounding the doctor's departure and she must hope that Liv will have the time to brood and that suspicions will resurface.

'I see that you still do the lion's share of the work,' Rosie says to Emmy, finding her alone in the kitchen before lunch on Boxing Day. 'Pity about old Betty. Heart, isn't it? A bit rough and ready but a good worker. You must miss her terribly. Liv certainly trades on your good nature.'

'Liv works just as hard as I do,' says Em calmly.

'You've always been easy on her,' laughs Rosie. 'And she takes it for granted. Of course, what she says is true.'

'What *does* she say?' asks Emmy after a pause – and Rosie smiles to herself.

'Oh that Mo isn't *her* mother,' she says lightly. 'That she couldn't afford to live anywhere else. Still it's a bit hard that you have to support your mother *and* your . . . and Liv.' She laughs. 'I nearly said "your sister" except that she isn't. Any more than Mo is her mother, as she's so ready to point out.'

'Is she?' says Em – and falls silent.

Rosie hopes that resentment will begin to stir in Emmy's heart. She sees that Emmy is calmer, that the rages and depressions of the middle life seem to be hauling off and she can see, too, that desperate remedies are called for if she is to succeed in her old policy of divide and rule. Unfortunately there is so little time and so little material with which to work.

\*       \*       \*

'Well I must say,' says Roop as they drive home, 'Liv didn't seem that worked up about the doctor. I didn't get a single rise out of her and she wasn't rude to me once. It was really quite dull. All that food and drink wasted.'

Roop likes to see a return on any outgoing. He especially likes to see a return on his very rare gestures of generosity.

'Mmm,' says Rosie thoughtfully. 'Of course, it *was* Christmas. They'd probably vowed to be on their best behaviour. And Mo's failing. It'll be her last Christmas for certain and I expect the girls were determined not to let anything upset her.'

Roop is distracted from thoughts of his dismal Christmas by the more cheerful thoughts of Mo's death.

'She's taking her time,' he says. 'To be quite honest it would be kinder to hit her on the head and have done.'

Rosie toys with the idea of saying, 'Please, Roop. She *is* my mother,' but knows it is far too late for such niceties.

'Tell me again,' she asks instead, 'how much we've been offered for first refusal?'

The house seems quiet after Rosie and Roop have left. Mo is tucked up for the night and Emmy and Liv sit beside what is left of the drawing-room fire. For some while they sit in silence, an air of constraint between them. It is Liv, who has been doing some serious thinking, who breaks this silence.

'Rosie says that it was you who told her that my "doctor friend",' she repeats Rosie's phrase with disgust, 'had left. Did you?'

'No,' says Emmy at once, staring Liv straight in the eye. 'We didn't discuss him. I never mentioned him at all.'

'Then how does she know about it?' asks Liv.

Emmy sees all the old misunderstandings starting up again and feels desperate. 'I don't know,' she cries, 'but it wasn't me. Please Liv. Don't start this all over again. I can't bear it.'

'No, no,' says Liv soothingly. 'I'm not starting anything. But I'm beginning to see a shred of light.'

'On what?' asks Em.

'On many things,' says Liv grimly. 'She told me these things because she's trying to cause trouble. Did she try to make trouble with you?'

Em is quiet for a moment. 'She said that you didn't pull your weight,' she says at last. 'I disagreed and she said that you took everything for granted. That you'd said Mo wasn't *your* mother and there was nowhere else you could live so cheaply. She said that it was bad luck that I was obliged to support you and Mo.'

'Well, so it is,' says Liv.

'I don't see it like that,' says Em. 'I couldn't have managed without you.'

'Em,' says Liv, 'why does Rosie want to make trouble between us?'

'She's always been like it, I suppose,' says Em, shrugging. 'From the beginning. We were jealous of her . . . What are you getting at?'

'I'm not sure yet,' says Liv slowly, 'but there's something in my mind. I'm working on it.'

'But why should she?' persists Em. 'Make trouble, I mean. What's the point?'

'When she was here last,' says Liv, still slowly, 'Rosie told me that you were jealous of me. She said that she'd noticed it even when she was little. That you were jealous that I got engaged first. She even mentioned our silly weekend, implying that you dreamed up the idea. She said that it was your idea that we went rushing off to London. She implied that, in your menopausal fits of depression you might still . . . do things, if you were jealous.'

Emmy stares at Liv, open-mouthed. 'You're joking,' she says. 'She said that? *Why*? I wasn't jealous when you got engaged. We had lots of fun. And we dreamed up that weekend together. Anyway,' she cries as Livy's words sink in, 'what does she mean by *things*?'

'She was implying,' says Livy, 'that you sent the anonymous letter and made that telephone call and I was foolish enough, then, to give the idea house room.'

Em closes her eyes. 'Am I hearing this right?' she enquires of no one in particular.

'She wants me to believe you ruined my life,' says Livy. Her face is angry.

'But she doesn't *know* about the letter and the phone call,' says Emmy, confused. 'Sorry. I'm not with this.'

'I think she knows,' says Liv, staring straight ahead. 'Do you know what she said? When we were talking about you being jealous of me, I asked her, *"How do you know? You were just a child."* And she said, *"Children notice everything,"* and mentioned a few things she'd overheard so as to give credence to her lies about you. I think she *did* overhear things. Important things. You and I talked about that weekend we had. Our fling. She could have heard us. Enough to write that letter.'

'But *why*?' cries Emmy. 'For God's sake *why*? What was she? Ten? Eleven?'

'I don't know why,' says Liv. 'I just know it. I've got a feeling.'

'And what about the phone call?' demands Emmy. 'How could she have known about the abortion? *I* certainly never breathed a word to her.'

'But it was talked about in this house.'

'Not when Rosie was here,' says Emmy with certainty. 'When you had those terrible pains and we discussed a hysterectomy, Rosie wasn't here. I know she wasn't. I remember simply because Alice was here on her own, without Rosie and Roop for once. I remember Alice wandering about . . .'

Her voice dies away. She is remembering something else;

a whispered conversation and her own terror '. . . *There's nothing really wrong is there? Is it because of the abortion? . . .'* and the feeling that someone was outside in the hall; a shadow? The flick of a skirt?

Em looks up to see Liv watching her. The expression on Liv's face frightens her and she swallows a little and shakes her head.

'Surely not?' she whispers. 'Surely . . . ? But why?'

'I don't know,' says Liv softly. 'I don't know yet. But I'm going to find out.'

# 15

Through the short days and long evenings of winter, Emmy and Liv try to piece together the truth. Whilst Mo dozes, stretched out on the sofa, the girls search their memories for clues. Heads together, voices low lest they disturb Mo, they try to resurrect the past.

'We must try to remember everything,' insists Liv when Emmy shakes her head hopelessly. 'Each little detail is important.'

'It's so long ago,' sighs Emmy, worn out with disturbed nights and anxious days.

Mo has had the flu and is very weak again.

'I've been thinking,' murmurs Liv. 'I think that we could trace all our troubles back to Rosie. Do you remember how Mo and Fa used to get to know things? Things that you and I knew but no one else? It seemed logical for us to believe that one of *us* had sneaked. I think it was Rosie.' She looks at Em stonily. 'Stop trying to think of excuses for her. Stop saying *"she was just a child"*. You and I were children when we tried to *kill her.*'

The words hang in the silence which is weighty and thick. It seems to press down upon them as they huddle together. Emmy glances instinctively towards Mo, who slumbers on peacefully.

'We tried to kill her,' whispers Livy relentlessly, 'because we hated her. She got us into trouble and Mo and Fa seemed to love her more than they loved us. She was their child. She was entitled to both of them. The Little Princess, remember? We were jealous. Jealous enough to kill.'

The whispering voice is silent and the silence comes closer again. Emmy remembers the berry in her pocket; her thumb and finger roll against each other as she thinks of it. Liv can feel the hot sun on her back, burning through the Aertex shirt.

'The berry wouldn't stay in her mouth,' whispers Em. 'It came trickling out with her dribble.'

'Boswell wouldn't keep still,' mutters Liv. 'I tried to hold him down but he scratched me.'

Mo stirs and mumbles upon the sofa and the two women by the fire draw closer together; the flames leap high and tall shadows dance across the walls; the cats curl up – two on chairs, one on the hearth rug – the frosty white of their fur tinged with gold in the firelight.

'I think that Rosie was jealous of us,' murmurs Liv. 'Especially after we started boarding school. She had Mo and Fa all to herself for nearly five years and then we came back and spoiled things. Try to think. We've got to remember . . .'

'Remember our party?' Em smiles a little. 'How thrilled we were with our dresses. Our first grown-up party. We wouldn't let Rosie stay up for dinner . . .'

Her smile fades a little and she falls silent, slowly remembering the series of incidents after the party; the rows that sprang up between her and Liv; the items that went missing . . .

'See?' hisses Liv, watching her. 'See what I mean?'

'Are you suggesting,' asks Em softly, 'that it was because of something like that, like not being allowed to stay up for dinner, that she wrote the letter?'

'Yes,' says Liv. 'That's *exactly* what I'm suggesting.'

'You honestly think she ruined our lives because of some childish whim? Because she was thwarted or jealous?'

'Emmy,' whispers Liv, 'we would have *killed* her because of our jealousy.'

'But we were ten years old,' protests Emmy. 'I accept that she might have done those things *then* because of jealousy but why should she make that telephone call *now* when she's forty-five? She can't *still* be jealous of us.'

'There's a reason,' mutters Liv. 'I know it. Give me time.'

Mo wakes suddenly and cries out, struggling with her rugs. Emmy rises to help her but Liv sits on, staring into the flames.

Rosie and Roop watch and wait. Rosie knows that she has been clumsy and curses herself but she no longer fears that Mo could be influenced to change her will. No doctor could possibly pronounce Mo in her right mind unless he were very prejudiced indeed, so Rosie is able to relax. She still fears Alice; but Alice is far away and they rarely hear from her and after all, reasons Rosie, what does Alice actually *know*? Nothing concrete, nothing she can prove. Nevertheless, Rosie tries to think of ways of actually silencing Alice for good. Perhaps there might be something which could be used to blackmail her daughter . . . ? Alice's room gives up no secrets although Rosie searches it very thoroughly. Nobody telephones her; nobody writes to her. Rosie broods on this whilst Roop fumes about the length of time it is taking Mo to die. He is terrified that his developer might find another desirable site and withdraw his offer.

In the middle of February there is a calm warm spell. The sun shines and green shoots can be seen, thrusting their way through the cold earth. Mo is better, though still frail, and she enjoys short drives in the car and the occasional half an hour in the summerhouse in the sunshine. After a few days of these little treats, she feels stronger although she is as confused as ever. Often she mistakes Livy for Pamela – and indeed Livy has a look of her aunt – and occasionally she thinks Emmy is her own mother but she is happy enough.

This morning the sun is bright and there is a black-bird singing in the garden. Mo wakes from her strange dreams and wonders where everyone is. Most mornings, after breakfast, she has a little nap to recover from the tiring process of dressing and eating and this morning she has been dozing in her armchair. Her padded knickers are wet and she removes them, dropping them on the floor, pulling up the long woollen socks which are sagging round her thin ankles, smoothing down her pleated skirt. She feels lively, quite strong enough for a walk, and collecting together one or two essentials – Fa's old cardigan, a tweed skirt – which she places carefully over her arm, she potters out on to the landing. She can hear the sound of a Hoover from below and she smiles gently. People will be busy, she decides, too busy to be disturbed, too busy for walks. She descends slowly into the hall. The front door is locked and having struggled ineffectually with the locks and bolts she wanders away, down the corridor, past the kitchen where the washing machine hums and out of the garden door.

Down the drive she goes, tacking unsteadily from side to side, along the narrow lane, humming happily to herself. 'Over my shoulder goes *one* care'. She is in her slippers but the lane is quite dry. The breeze blowing up her pleated skirt is rather draughty but the sun on her back is warm. 'Over my shoulder go *two* cares'. She pauses to watch a robin in the hedge, her head on one side to catch his little song, then on she goes again. She is tiring now, shuffling a little. The things she has brought with her weigh heavily on her arm and she drops the tweed skirt on the narrow grass verge.

The first cottages of the village are to be seen and Mo presses on doggedly, breathing heavily as she hums. '*Over* my *shoulder* . . .'

It is unfortunate that the second cottage belongs to the village's Good Samaritan who is out in her garden keeping an eye on her plants, lest they should become too forward in this false spring, and hoping that someone will need her guidance and care before lunch. So far this morning she has not been lucky. The postman has been almost offensively in charge of his own life and the shoplady has been disinterested in how *she* dealt with *her* young daughter when she wanted to stay out late. Now she stands alert at the sound of the shuffling footsteps, hardly able to believe her eyes. Mo is dragging along, unaware of where she is, eyes fixed on the road as she hums tunelessly. The Good Samaritan leaps into action. Hurrying out into the lane, she seizes Mo gently by the arm.

'Whatever *are* you doing, Mrs Faringdon, dear?' she chides. 'You shouldn't be out all alone. What are those girls of yours up to, letting you wander off like this? Now come along. In we go.'

Mo peers up at her as she suffers herself to be led into the cottage and put into a comfortable chair.

'Now,' says the G.S., not *quite* able to hide her glee at being so signally needed. '*Now* . . . A nice warming drink. Sugar, I think. You'll be feeling weak after that long walk . . .'

She leafs through the telephone directory, one eye on Mo, who, having drunk her hot milk, sits smoothing Fa's cardigan over her skinny knees. Mo is frowning, shifting distressfully in the deep upholstered chair; she strains a little and then relaxes, smiling again.

'Yes indeed,' the G.S. is saying soothingly to a distraught Liv. 'Here in my sitting room. Walking down the lane on her own. Good thing I recognised her. Yes, second cottage on the left. She's exhausted, of course . . .'

Emmy is already on her way in the car. She parks and runs in, hardly stopping to knock.

'Oh Mo,' she says, falling on her knees beside her chair. 'You *did* give us a fright.'

'I *do* wonder,' says Mo's Good Samaritan gently, 'whether such a responsibility isn't becoming just a *little* too much for you, Emily dear. I remember when my own dear mother became ill, you know, and the real question, here, is "what is best for *her*?" Oh, I understand just how you and your sister feel . . .'

Emmy swallows and listens meekly to these strictures. She would like to give Mo a good smack; instead she helps her to her feet, feeling murderously inclined towards the G.S. and wondering if the man who fell among thieves had the same reaction when he began to recover.

'No, don't thank me, dear,' the G.S. is saying in quiet, saintly tones. 'Anyone would have done the same, but *do* think carefully, dear, about what . . .'

There is a sharp intake of breath and Emmy, who is edging Mo towards the door, glances back over her shoulder. Her eyes follow the transfixed gaze of the G.S and she sees a large spreading wet patch on the chair where Mo has been sitting. The back of Mo's skirt is wet, too, but she seems unaware of the discomfort.

'I'm so sorry,' murmurs Emmy to the G.S. whose eyes, fixed on the seat, seem to be in danger of falling out onto the carpet. 'Perhaps you gave her something to drink. Very unwise. Come along, Mo. Thank you so much.'

Back in the car, she laughs and laughs. Mo, sitting on a prudently placed mackintosh, smiles happily. '*Over* my shoulder goes it *all*,' she sings threadily. On the way home, Em stops to pick up the tweed skirt which has been run over by the large muddy wheel of a tractor.

Mo's adventure seems to set her back. She sinks into a

confused, tired condition and rarely leaves her room. She gets a chest infection and her breathing is laboured and she eats less and less. Emmy and Liv both believe that the end cannot be far off and they are afraid to leave her alone.

'It really took it out of her,' says Emmy sadly, 'that walk into the village. If only we'd been more on the ball.'

'I know,' says Liv, 'but we couldn't lock her in. And it was such a lovely day. I think she enjoyed herself.'

Emmy chuckles, despite her guilt and anxiety. 'I'm sure she did. But I think it used up all her last reserves. I did so hope that she'd have the summer, having survived another winter.'

'We don't know that she won't,' points out Liv. 'She's been really poorly before but she's made a comeback. Let's not give up just yet.'

Mo revives a little. They have a surprise visit from Betty who is driven up to the house by Jackie, down from London for a few days. Betty spends most of her time in London with Jackie and her husband now. She looks old and tired and ill but Mo recognises her at once and the four of them spend a happy morning together. Jackie is cheerful and amusing and Betty makes light of her troubles, so that it is quite like old times. Mo seems revitalised by the visit and Emmy and Liv begin to hope that, with a lot of love and care, she might yet see the summer through. Her big sunny bedroom that she shared with Fa is made as comfortable as possible and the girls spend the spring days there with her, turn and turn about, or together. Liv has a jigsaw puzzle going on the little table by the window and Em's knitting lives in a bag by a small armchair. They read to her, talk quietly to each other whilst she sleeps and carry their meals upstairs to eat with her.

One afternoon, late in April, Mo stirs, opens her eyes and smiles vaguely about her. Sunshine pours in at the tall windows and the world is full of the sound of birdsong and the distant growl of traffic.

'Hi, Mo,' says Liv, who is doing a crossword. 'Good timing. How about a cuppa?'

Mo's gaze drifts away around the room and her brow wrinkles a little. 'Dark,' she murmurs faintly. 'So dark, darling.'

Liv stares at her, stands up and runs out on to the landing. 'Em,' she screams through the silent house. 'Emmy! Come quickly!'

Em takes the stairs two at a time, still clutching the potato peeler, but Liv has already gone back into the bedroom and is holding Mo's hand. Mo's eyes are shut again and she breathes with difficulty. Emmy falls on her knees beside the bed and takes the other thin old hand.

'Mo,' she says, pleadingly. 'Mo . . .'

They are silent, waiting. As she spirals down into death, Mo is vouchsafed a vision. In their Elysian field, Fa and Mother and Pamela are waiting for her. They hold out their hands and Mo sees that they are each holding a glass which is full of bright frothing liquid. They appear to be celebrating and Mo knows exactly what they are celebrating and smiles contentedly.

'Co-ming,' she calls in her cracked old voice. '*Cooo*-ming.' As she sinks down towards them, she has a horrid feeling that she has forgotten something vital. What can it be? The girls, seeing her struggle back towards life, lean forward, hoping that she will recognise them for the last time and say goodbye. She attempts to free her hands and pats feebly about her on the bed until she feels the familiar shape.

'*Cooo*-ming,' she calls again . . . and falls back dead on her pillows, the flask clutched to her breast.

# 16

Mo's death does not find Rosie unprepared. She has already had the foresight to approach the executor of Mo's will, who is the son of one of Fa's colleagues at the bank. He is unwilling to discuss the future administration of the estate with one of the beneficiaries but Rosie speaks so movingly of his father's friendship with Fa that he agrees to a meeting. It is clear that she knows the contents of the will but he is rather disturbed when Rosie makes her intention known to him.

'It's been their home for so long,' he murmurs, 'and they have been wonderful with Mrs Faringdon.'

'It was my home, too,' Rosie reminds him with a nice blend of wistful sadness. 'But don't you see, it's much too big for them and so expensive to run. They have hardly any income and I'm afraid they will stop looking after themselves properly.' She sighs and shakes her head worriedly. 'They'll stop eating sensibly and they simply won't keep themselves warm once they don't have Mo to worry about.'

'Oh . . .' He is completely taken in. 'Oh, I see.'

'Now, if we can sell the place we can buy them a cosy easy-to-run cottage or a flat and they'll have the rest of their share of the money to live on. Now, *don't* you think that's much more sensible?'

She smiles at him and he is touched by her charm and the care she has for her sisters.

'Much more sensible,' he agrees, 'but I'm not certain they will see it like that.'

'You must back me up,' she says. 'I know them so well. Of course it will be difficult for them. Of *course* it will. Do you think I don't feel it, too?' She swallows a little and touches a dainty handkerchief to the corner of her eye. 'I shall have to steel myself . . . I expect you think I'm very hard . . .'

'Good Heavens no!' He is getting up, pressing his intercom, saying, 'Two coffees, Jane,' and making inarticulate protesting noises while he waits for Rosie to collect herself.

'So sorry,' she says, smiling at him gratefully. 'Do forgive me. I still find it hard to believe that dear, darling Mo won't be with us much longer . . .'

'Quite,' he says hastily, pressing her shoulder with a reassuring hand. 'Quite. Please don't distress yourself.'

'The very least I can do,' says Rosie, tucking away her handkerchief and making an obvious effort to calm herself, 'is to look after Emmy and Liv properly. I know they'll fight me.' She sighs sadly. 'It's so hard when people misunderstand one.'

'Ah,' he says, relieved. 'Here is Jane with our coffee. Thank you.' He waits for the door to close again and smiles encouragingly at Rosie. 'Now, you must tell me exactly what you've got in mind . . .'

He makes notes, nodding sagely, seeing the sense of it all and promising that he won't weaken under pressure.

'But you must let it come from me,' she warns him. 'I know the will must be read but they will be far too upset at that time to take it in. It would be too cruel. I must pick my moment. I know you'll understand.'

'Of course,' he says, touched by her concern for her sisters.

'I'm counting on you,' she says roguishly as they part and

he presses her hand speakingly and promises that she may do so with absolute confidence.

After the funeral, Roop wants to act immediately but Rosie stays his hand. It is clear that Emmy and Liv have never considered that they might have to leave the house. They have listened to a reading of the will, knowing already that the house and its contents – apart from the girls' personal belongings – must be divided three ways. Yet it has not occurred to them that Rosie, who has a big warm comfortable house of her own, will require them to move out.

'Why wait?' chafes Roop. 'We've waited long enough. Everything's ready to roll.'

'I know,' says Rosie. 'I just want them to understand what we intend to do. They're too shocked at the moment to take it in.'

What she really means is that she wants them to be fully conscious when she deals the blow, so that their suffering will in no way be mitigated. In this one last act she will revenge herself for all the slights and jibes that she – and Roop – have received over the years. She wants to savour the look on their faces when it finally dawns upon them that they will have to leave the house.

In the weeks that follow the funeral, Emmy and Livy spend long hours sitting in the summerhouse doing nothing. They are able to share their grief and their mourning takes a natural healing course. They weep when the mood takes them and neither tells the other to brace up or offers false comfort. Slowly they recover as they sit in the sun.

'I feel like a marionette that's had its strings cut,' says Emmy, sagging limply in her chair. 'All my energy has gone. Simply standing up is an effort.'

'We're tired,' says Liv. 'We've been on the go for years.

Suddenly we've stopped and we've realised how knackered we are.'

'She was a full-time job,' admits Emmy. 'I could have cheerfully murdered her on occasions but I miss her so much.'

'The great thing about Mo,' says Liv, 'was her jolliness. She never moaned or whined, did she?'

'Only when she lost that damned flask,' chuckles Em.

They sit together, exhausted, staring out.

'If it weren't for that bloody road,' says Liv, 'it would be lovely. *Don't* tell me to close my eyes and pretend that it's the sea.'

'Now that Mo . . . Now that we've got more time,' begins Emmy, trying to sound a little more animated, 'we can sort out the house and the garden. There's so much I want to do. And one of the things is to move this summerhouse.'

'If you try to shift it,' Livy tells her, 'it'll fall to pieces.'

'OK then,' says Emmy. 'We'll buy a new one.'

Liv snorts mirthlessly. 'Taking buttons are they?'

'We'll sell something. Or borrow some money. It'll give us something to think about, to plan for. We can't just sit here, staring mindlessly at nothing.'

'Why not?' says Liv. 'I *like* sitting here staring mindlessly at nothing. If it weren't for that bloody road . . .'

'In the little yard,' muses Emmy. 'Mo always said that's where Fa wished he'd put it. In the little yard. Over the old well . . .'

'We ought to be getting on with the inventory,' says Liv, not moving.

'What's the point?' asks Emmy. 'We all know what's in the house. It's been there long enough.'

'Something to do with probate,' says Liv, yawning.

They sit in silence in the sun, too tired to stand up and go back to the house for some lunch. They are unused to freedom and time hangs heavily on their hands but they lack the energy to tackle the tasks that still await them.

'OK,' says Rosie. 'The time's come.'

'Thank God for that,' says Roop irritably. 'You've taken long enough.'

'Can you imagine the local reaction,' asks Rosie patiently, 'if we'd thrown them out right after Mo died? We want local support when those contractors go in, not a whispering campaign. *"They turned those poor old women out to convert that house? Right after their mother died. Hardly cold in her grave. Got a big house in London, too. Greed. That's all it was. And we've got all the extra traffic coming through these lanes . . ."* Is that what you want being whispered in the village and in the town? Do you want prospective buyers to hear that when they go into the local for a pint and a nose round? They'll be afraid that if they buy they'll be ostracised.'

'The locals aren't *that* fond of Emmy and Liv,' mutters Roop defensively.

'They would have been if we'd thrown them out straight after the funeral.'

'The funeral was months ago.' Roop is still feeling rebellious. He is afraid of losing all that lovely money – and he hates being in the wrong. 'Mo died in April. It's nearly August.'

'That's right,' says Rosie affably. 'That's what I said, didn't I? Now's the time.'

Roop swallows down his sense of grievance. He imagines the girls' faces when Rosie tells them that she is about to dispossess them and his spirits rise.

'I must say,' he says, good humour almost restored, 'that I'm longing to see their faces.'

'Well, you'll have to wait,' says Rosie. 'I'm doing this one on my own.'

Roop looks ludicrously disappointed. 'But why?' he cries,

like a child who has been denied a treat. 'Why can't I come too?'

Rosie is silent for moment. She knows that this meeting is going to be a tricky one and she doesn't want Roop standing by, rubbing his hands with glee, unable to contain his delight or putting in his two pennyworth. No. This scene is to be played strictly between Liv, Emmy and herself. She thinks very quickly.

'Look,' she says, 'this is just the opening round. They won't even believe me this time. They'll be quite sure that I won't have the power to throw them out. They think it's two against one. See? This is just a casual opening salvo. You'll be there for the big one. I promise.'

Roop is unconvinced. He wants to see comprehension and horror dawning on those two faces who have laughed and mocked and sneered at him.

'It won't be the same,' he says sullenly – but Rosie stands firm.

'Just make sure,' he says crossly, as a parting shot, 'that they're getting on with that inventory.'

Rosie waits until after lunch before she begins. She has noticed evidence of industry; weeding and digging in the garden; a step ladder and pots of paint in the drawing room. She smiles to herself and pokes about, making certain that the more valuable items of furniture are still in their usual places. When they have finished lunch and have coffee before them, Rosie takes a deep breath and smiles upon them.

'I'm so pleased,' she says mendaciously, 'to see you both looking a little better. You were looking absolutely exhausted last time. It looks as if you've both been busy, too. It's a good sign but, you know, it's absolutely unnecessary. The place will sell perfectly well without you doing it up.'

She waits, her eyes on their faces, drinking in their puzzled expressions. She was right to have denied Roop the treat. He would have been too eager; hurrying to make the points; too unsubtle.

'What d'you mean?' asks Liv, inevitably. 'Sell perfectly well? What are you talking about?'

Rosie evinces a reaction which is a perfect blend of surprise and anxiety. 'Well . . . The house. You must have realised that it has to be sold up?'

'Sold up? But why?' asks Emmy. It's ridiculous but suddenly she is afraid. 'Why should we sell? We live here. It's our home.'

Rosie laughs lightly. 'I know that,' she says gently. 'But you've seen Mo's will. It has to be split between the three of us.'

'But you've got a house,' says Emmy. 'You don't need another one.'

Liv sits silent. She knows now that Rosie is about to deal the hardest blow of all and she rages inwardly that she has allowed the months to pass without pursuing her theory regarding Rosie's past betrayals.

'That's true,' agrees Rosie, readily. 'We don't need the house but we *do* need the cash. Things haven't been too good for us lately.'

'And what are *we* supposed to do?' asks Liv quietly.

Rosie raises her eyebrows. 'Whatever you like,' she says. 'There will be plenty of money to buy you a cottage or a flat and a good sum left over to invest. Goodness! Don't tell me you haven't even discussed it yet.' She laughs affectionately. 'You *are* a hopeless pair. Never mind. Think about it now. Where would you like to go? Country or town? Cottage or flat?'

'Try to remember,' says Em quietly, 'that this is *my* home. We have inherited it through *my* mother.'

'But *my* father,' snaps Liv, still furious with herself for not having seen this coming, 'paid the mortgages and the debts. There wouldn't *be* a house to sell without him.'

'Not *quite* the point,' cries Emmy, who feels nothing but terror at the thought of being dispossessed; her links with her past snapped irrevocably.

'*Exactly* the point,' snaps Liv, hurt that Emmy has excluded her from right of ownership, wondering what Rosie's legal position is.

'Girls, girls,' cries Rosie, hands pressed girlishly over her ears. 'Not all that again. Anyway, *my* mother, *my* father, remember.'

The other two fall silent, united again by this claim.

'I shan't go,' says Em, bravely. 'What about you, Liv? How do you feel?'

'Of course I don't want to leave,' says Liv. 'You know that.'

Rosie sees the subtle difference in the two answers. She knows the doubts are sown in Liv's mind and she smiles at Em.

'I understand how you feel,' she says. 'Of course I do. Although I think it's crazy for you to think that you could afford to go on living here. Still, that's your business. If you insist on staying then you'll just have to buy me out.'

'Buy you out?' Emmy frowns.

'Look,' says Rosie, as if she's explaining an easy sum to a backward child, 'a third of this house and its contents are legally mine. That's fair, isn't it? Well, I need the money. I know you think Roop and I are rolling in it but we aren't. And even if we were, why shouldn't I have my share? Mo and Fa were my legal parents, which is more than can be said for either of you. I'm entitled to my share of the estate. If you want to go on living here then you'll have to raise my share and buy me out.'

She sits back, as though exhausted by her efforts to make Em understand, and glances at Liv.

'What she means,' says Liv, 'is that we get everything valued, divide the sum by three and pay her one third.'

'Then that's what we'll do,' cries Em desperately – but she looks frightened.

Rosie shakes her head, amused. 'Have you any idea of what kind of money we're talking here?' she asks. 'Do you think you'd be able to raise a mortgage of a hundred thousand or so? And even if you could, how would you pay it back?'

'A hundred *thousand*? This house is worth that much?' asks Emmy, stunned.

'Three times that much,' says Liv. 'A hundred thousand would be her portion.'

'I don't believe it,' says Emmy flatly. 'It can't be true. Can it, Liv?'

'Oh, yes,' says Liv, watching Rosie's face. 'If that's what she says I think we can take it as read that it's true.'

# 17

When she is gone Livy and Em sit where she has left them, at the kitchen table. Em is shaken but, as yet, refuses to believe that Rosie can turn them out.

'It's two against one,' she says, over and over again. 'She doesn't need another house. No court would turn us out of our home.'

Liv's brain is active, worrying around the problem. She has no doubt that Rosie has checked and double checked but there might be a loophole. She gets up and goes out to telephone the executor. Primed by Rosie he is kind but firm; their sister is well within her rights, he tells her. There will be plenty of money to buy themselves another home.

'But we want to stay in this one,' she tells him.

He laughs a little reprovingly and points out the advantages of a smaller, more economical establishment.

'But this is our *home*,' cries Livy, losing control. 'My sister's family have been here for more than a hundred years. She was born here. So was Mo.'

'I have to point out,' he says gently, 'that no provision has been made for you to continue to live in the house. Try not to be too inflexible in your outlook. Naturally it will be painful for you both to leave but one must remain forward looking. I think . . .'

Liv slams down the receiver and goes back to the kitchen.

Emmy is still sitting at the table and she stares up at her, hope dying in her face as she sees Liv's expression.

'What happened?' she asks fearfully.

'Rosie's right,' says Liv abruptly, sitting down. 'She has every right to turn us out. He doesn't give a shit that your family has been here for years or that it's home to us. He's on Rosie's side.'

'I'm not going,' says Em stubbornly. 'I won't. We'll have to raise the money somehow.'

Liv looks at her. She hears a note in Em's voice which worries her; a tinge of hysteria. Em's lips are pressed tightly together but she looks as if she might weep. Liv thinks quickly. She knows how deeply Em has been affected by Mo's death; how important it is for her to maintain her links with the past.

'We've got to think,' she says, trying to sound as calm as possible. 'There may be a way round it. It wouldn't surprise me if Rosie's somehow got at the worthy executor. Don't give up, Em.'

'I shan't,' says Em – but her voice is shaky. 'What can we do?'

'We can take independent advice,' says Liv thoughtfully. 'What we need is a nice friendly lawyer who won't charge us the earth.'

'I don't know any nice friendly lawyers,' says Em, trying for a lighter note. 'The only one I knew seduced my little sister.'

Liv looks at her for a long unsmiling moment. 'What a pity,' she says, 'that we got sidetracked from our detective work. Now if we had something on Rosie we might be in with a chance.'

'You mean if we could prove she made that telephone call?' Em sounds more hopeful.

'Something like that.' Livy is turning an idea over in her mind. 'We'll never be able to prove she wrote the letter or made the call. I think Alice was her informant about the abortion but she'd never admit to it. Or would she?'

'Alice is abroad,' Emmy reminds her. 'She may not be back for months. We can't wait that long.'

'No,' says Liv. 'So how would you feel about phoning your erstwhile nice friendly lawyer and asking him what really happened?'

Emmy stares at her, alarmed. 'You don't believe it was him, then?'

'No,' says Liv grimly. 'I think that if you could bring yourself to think back you'd find that you said or did something to upset our dear sister and she decided to get her own back.'

'But why didn't he fight it?' cries Em. 'He just went quietly away and I never saw him again. He never wrote or attempted an explanation.'

'How could he?' asks Liv scornfully. 'With Mo and Rosie screaming the place down and Fa threatening to report him to the Law Society if he ever contacted any of us again, how could he?'

'Mo saw him with her,' says Em, remembering. 'She was so kind to me but she was shocked and disgusted. I wouldn't believe her and she had to give me the details. She said that his hand . . . Anyway, it's too late to go into it now.'

'No it isn't,' says Liv firmly. 'He'd had too much to drink. I think Rosie manipulated him into a compromising situation and made sure that Mo saw exactly what she wanted her to see.'

'But why?' cries Em. 'It's unbelievable. She was only – what? – fourteen?'

'Old enough,' says Liv. '*Think*, Em. Had you upset her?'

Emmy puts her elbows on the table and shields her eyes with her hands. She remembers the Christmas scene and Rosie showing off as she dances about, posturing and pouting. She remembers the trip to Midnight Mass and recalls that Rosie almost falls asleep during the service . . .

'I pushed her into the car on his lap,' she recounts slowly. 'It was all a bit of a squeeze and, when we got home she made a great fuss about having been on his lap . . . She wriggled about like a tart and flapped her eyelashes at him and I . . . I told her that she was still a little girl and not to be so silly. Something like that.'

'In front of him?' asks Liv sharply.

'Yes, in front of him,' says Em impatiently. 'He laughed and she went very red and rushed indoors . . . and that's it. Can't think of anything else.' She looks at Liv and shakes her head at Liv's expression. 'Oh come on. You're not going to tell me that because of a put-down she staged a seduction scene and ruined my life.'

'I think it's very likely,' says Liv. 'You just refuse to accept the type of character she is.'

'It's difficult to accept that your sister is some kind of psychotic,' agrees Em. 'After all, it wasn't a big scene. I was sharp with her, yes, but it was nothing to the fuss *you* made when she cracked that little china box that had belonged to your mum. You slapped her good and proper, then, if I recall and called her all sorts of names.'

Liv sits up straight, her eyes shining. 'Well done, Em,' she says. 'You've done it. I've thought and thought about what made her send that letter. That's what it was. The little box. God, I was cross. And she couldn't sneak because Mo always told her that she mustn't touch our things.'

'Then she *is* mad,' says Em flatly. 'And she's still trying to wreck our lives for tiny little things like that?'

'Listen,' says Liv, leaning across the table. 'Try to remember how we were when we tried to kill her. OK, we were kids but we felt strongly enough to wish her dead. Think about it. *Remember* it. Then you'll know how *she* feels. Try to understand it, Em, or we can't fight her.'

There is a silence.

'I feared her,' says Em slowly. 'Mo and Fa were so obsessed by her. She belonged to both of them in a way that we never could. I envied her that. I envied the way she'd climb into bed with them and feel that she belonged. I loved Fa but I couldn't do that. I felt that they must love her better, simply because she was *theirs*.'

'The thing was,' says Liv, 'that once *she* came along they weren't so hell bent on pleasing *us*. We manipulated them until she arrived and then things changed. We got told off, smacked. It was all *her* fault. That's how we saw it.'

'But when we grew up and began to accept *her*,' goes on Em, '*she* began to resent *us*. But why still now?'

'She likes to be on top,' says Liv, 'and we've never given her the satisfaction of feeling that she is. We've been unimpressed by her belongings and, let's face it, we've given Roop hell.'

'And so now she's going to make us homeless,' finishes Em.

'Something like that,' agrees Liv. 'I can't forgive her for the phone call. My God, how she must hate me!'

'Us,' says Em. 'She hates us and is going to do her best to get us out. Could a lawyer help us?'

Liv looks at her and the same thought is in both their minds.

'Do you think he's with the same law firm?' asks Em at last.

'Probably,' says Liv. 'Why not? If not, they can probably tell you where he is. And when you speak to him, make it clear that you've found out that it wasn't his fault and see how he reacts.'

'Oh God,' says Em. 'How can I? It's been so long. Oh God . . .'

'Stop jittering,' says Liv. 'Get on to directory enquiries. It's worth a try.'

\*       \*       \*

'So how did they take it?' asks Roop. He is still sulking a little but he can't resist asking.

'You shall come next time,' promises Rosie. 'Like I said, they didn't take it in. Wouldn't believe me. Quite funny, really.'

'Well, they've damn well got to believe it,' blusters Roop. 'I hope you made it clear that they've *got* to get out. My chap won't wait much longer . . .'

'You see,' says Rosie smugly. 'That's exactly why I said you couldn't come. It's no good approaching it like that. They'll dig their heels in and it will take years to get them out. We've got to take it carefully. We want it on our terms.'

'Right's on our side,' says Roop crossly – but he sees Rosie's point. 'What next, then?'

'We'll give them a week or so,' says Rosie thoughtfully. 'They'll probably try to get legal advice. Not that it matters. They haven't got a leg to stand on.'

'Must we have this farce?' grumbles Roop.

'We'll go down together,' promises Rosie. 'I want you to see Emmy's face when she realises that Mo's bureau will have to be sold. It's much too valuable to allow her to keep it. It'll be fun, you'll see.'

Roop laughs, albeit unwillingly. 'No more Pigling Bland,' he says grimly.

'Oh, no,' agrees Rosie softly. 'No more Pigling Bland.'

Emmy's lawyer is at first amazed to hear her voice and then wary. He is one of the partners now and has a wife, three grown-up children and several small grandchildren. He is filled with terror lest she has telephoned to make trouble but her first words allay his fears somewhat.

'Mo died last spring,' she tells him. 'You remember Mo? My mother? And I suddenly felt that it was time to put the record straight. I never really believed that story, you know. My sister set you up, didn't she?'

His relief is so great that he feels he might faint, yet he retains enough wits to know that it is risky to have such a conversation on the office telephone.

'I'm sure you'll understand,' he says cautiously, 'if I say that I can't go in to details now. But yes. What you say is quite true. It was frightful. I tried to tell myself that she was deluded. Mad. But it was a terrible shock.'

'My sister is evil,' says Emmy flatly. 'It's taken us a while to face the facts. Could we meet? I'd like to talk to you.'

The lawyer hesitates. Might it be a trap? Will the younger sister suddenly be produced and start screaming accusations? In an age when the Salem witch hunts seem to be making a comeback and children are encouraged by over zealous social workers or hypnotism to accuse their innocent parents of violation, anything could happen. Suing seems to have become a national sport and huge compensation for all sorts of preposterous claims is awarded recklessly.

'Please,' Emmy is saying. 'You can choose the time and place. Please trust me. The fact is that, now Mo and Fa are dead, Rosie is trying to get Livy and me thrown out of the house. We need help. But really I just want to say that I don't believe anything Rosie said. I hope you can forgive me. All of us.'

She sounds sincere and, quite suddenly, he decides to take a chance. Her voice has reminded him of happier days, when you could smoke on aeroplanes and pat a girl on the shoulder without being arraigned for sexual harassment.

'It would be very pleasant to see you again,' he says. 'Did you have anywhere in mind?'

'Look,' says Emmy hopefully. 'Could you come and see us here? There's just Livy and me. We'd love to see you. She and I have lived here with Mo for years, you know. Rosie managed to ruin Liv's life as well as mine. Please come.'

He is flattered by the insinuation that her life was ruined. His own has been happy enough, if lacking excitement, and he wonders briefly what life with Emmy would have been like. Suddenly he is curious to see her again; to see what ravages time has made on her dark prettiness. Her voice still sounds quite young . . .

'Very well,' he agrees. 'I'll come and see you both. Now you'll have to remind me exactly where you are . . .'

'He's coming,' says Em, pale with excitement. 'I can't believe it. He said it *was* Rosie.'

'Of course it was,' says Liv scornfully. 'Poor chap. Fancy having something like that hanging round your neck all your life.'

'We'll be able to put that right,' says Em. 'At least it's not too late for that. God, when I think of it . . . I'd like to murder Rosie.'

'Well,' says Livy thoughtfully. 'We almost achieved it once. Who's to say we shouldn't have another try?'

# 18

He arrives promptly, driving a smart car, and pauses on the gravel to look about him before turning towards the house. Em has been watching from the breakfast room and she hurries out, her heart knocking hard against her breast bone. They exchange rather breathless greetings, each trying to recognise the person they once knew whilst trying not to stare.

He is shorter than she remembers but his hair is still fair, though faded. He looks prosperous but there is a look of someone who works too hard for too long; an urban pallor to his skin.

She looks strangely familiar to him though she is quite grey now and thin. With a sense of shock he realises that he is looking at Mo as she was when he first knew Emmy and memories of the whole dreadful business come rolling back.

'You look exactly like your mother,' he says, smiling at her. 'How odd.' He laughs a little and then grows serious. 'I hope you don't mind my saying that?' he asks quickly.

Emmy, who thinks of Mo as she was just before she died, is taken aback before she grasps that he is talking of Mo thirty-five years ago. Nevertheless it is a sobering concept.

'I miss her terribly,' she says. 'Look. This is really very good of you to come all this way . . .'

'Oh, not so very far,' he says. He knows quite surely that he has nothing to fear from her after all. 'It's changed a bit though, hasn't it? Surely the town didn't extend quite so far? And that motorway doesn't exactly contribute to your peace and quiet.'

Emmy grimaces. 'For God's sake don't mention the motorway to Liv. It's her *bête noire*. Come in and have a drink and meet her.'

There is something pleasant about having a man in the house again. It reminds Emmy and Liv of the happy times when the doctor sat in the kitchen drinking coffee and Mo and Pamela were alive. They become light-hearted, joking with each other and reminding him of the escapades the three of them had in London before the fateful Christmas.

Later, he tells them the truth about the Boxing Day scene with Rosie on the sofa. His voice is quiet and he is able to describe it unemotionally but with absolute exactness. He has been over it so many times in his own mind since then. Liv's face is grim and closed as she listens; Em watches his face and wonders if she will be able to hold back her tears. She sees now all that she has lost, all that might have been hers, and presently anger grows greater than her desire to weep. They talk at great length, discussing Rosie and her determination to see the house sold. He has no comfort to offer; legally, she is within her rights.

After lunch, Liv disappears into the kitchen whilst the other two wander out into the garden.

'I'm so glad that it's been cleared up,' he tells Emmy. 'It's been like a rather horrid stain on my life. I wish your parents could have known.'

'It's shocking,' Emmy's voice trembles, 'that you have had to live with it.'

'Well,' he sees her distress and attempts to comfort her, 'now that you and Liv know the truth I can forget it. If there's anything I can ever do . . .'

'That's very generous of you,' says Emmy, 'under the circumstances.' Her gut is twisted with the old love for him and she feels that she will die if he just walks away from her. 'If you think of anything that might help us . . . ?'

'Of course,' he says readily. 'Of course I will. Well, I suppose I ought to be getting on my way.'

'Oh, please,' cries Em desperately, 'please don't go just yet. Stay for tea. I've made a cake.' She attempts a light laugh. 'Now surely that's an offer you can't refuse?'

He looks at her intently and very sadly. 'I think it's best if I go,' he says. 'Forgive me, Emmy. It would be so easy to be very foolish. Thank you for today. It's meant far more than I can tell you.'

'At least,' she pleads, 'come and say goodbye to Livy.' Surely Livy will persuade him to stay; offer him tea or a drink? *'Please,'* she begs.

He hesitates, torn between her need and his own wisdom. He guesses how easy it might be to let things get out of hand; how pleasant it would be to take a run down here 'to see a client'; how tempting, when life was dull or demanding, to escape for a few hours. He knows that he might be able to juggle things accordingly so that his wife would never suspect; he knows, too, that the undivided attention of two women – one of whom is in love with him – would be a tremendous boost to his ego. How, though, would it be for Emmy? He sees the longing in her eyes and imagines how difficult it might become for her, waiting on his convenience or whim. How soon would it be before the waiting and hoping began to irk and annoy? No. It is best to stop it now with a quick clean cut.

He takes her hands and holds them tightly. 'It's no good, Emmy,' he says gently. 'We're thirty-five years too late. Say goodbye to Liv for me.'

He kisses her quickly and climbs into his car whilst she is still standing quite still, a hand to her cheek. Liv comes running out when she hears the car's engine and watches it go down the drive and out through the gateway. She looks quickly at Em who is still standing where he left her. Liv puts an arm round her shoulders but says nothing. She remembers how she felt in similar circumstances.

'Come,' she says at last. 'Come inside. I'll make some tea. No. I've had a better idea. I think we need a drink.'

They have a drink; several drinks. They go on drinking as the afternoon passes into evening. Emmy weeps a little, then she laughs, then she grows angry.

'I hate Rosie,' she says between set teeth. 'I hate her. If she comes here again I shall *kill* her.'

Truly, she speaks prophetically.

'Time for another visit,' says Rosie to Roop. 'Time to really put the boot in.'

They discuss how they might keep the lion's share of the more valuable pieces for themselves.

'If you can't agree on who has what,' says Roop, 'then the things have to be sold off. OK. So we get them away to be valued. Livy and Em won't have a clue what the pieces are worth. I know a chap who might be quite useful there.'

'The trouble is,' says Rosie, 'if they come visiting, they'll see them. Could be tricky.'

'Balls,' says Roop contemptuously. 'When do they ever come to see us? But if you're worried, we'll put them in the cottage for the time being. They'll never crawl all the way to the borders just to see us.'

'True,' says Rosie. 'But we'll have to allow them something or it will begin to look suspicious.'

'Annoying, isn't it?' says Roop. 'We should have done a proper recce. We'll have a code. If we're going to let them have something we'll give each other some kind of password.'

'Good idea,' says Rosie. 'Now what shall it be? Hang on, though. Which of us does the deciding?'

'You'd better,' says Roop rather reluctantly. 'It would be more natural.'

'OK,' agrees Rosie. 'I'll say something like, "Oh, yes, Mo – or Fa – would have wanted you to have that." Will that do?'

'Yes,' says Roop, unhappy at the thought of Emmy or Liv having anything at all. 'But don't be *too* generous.'

Rosie chuckles at such a ludicrous idea and pats him on the knee. 'Trust me,' she says.

Emmy and Liv, however, have been forewarned. The lawyer, as he is driving home, has gone over things carefully in his mind and he telephones next morning to warn them against various possible dangers. He tells Emmy that Mo might have wanted certain pieces to go to different daughters. She would have written the name in question on a label and attached it to the item. It might not be legally binding, he says, but it takes a brave person to set themselves up against the known wishes of the dead.

'But Mo didn't do anything of the kind,' says Emmy, delighted to hear his voice. 'It would never have occurred to her for a moment.'

'What a pity,' says the lawyer expressionlessly. 'Would Rosie recognise Mo's writing?'

There is a silence.

'Yes,' says Em slowly. 'Yes, I see.'

'Good. Right. Must get on. You can always leave a message with my secretary if you need me.'

Emmy pours herself a steadying gin. His voice has unsettled her, stirred up her old longings, but she knows there is no future in it. He will help her if he can but it will be no more than that. She must fight against a temptation to telephone on some pretext just so as to hear his voice.

'After all,' mutters Em, sipping. 'I have *some* pride.'

'Glad to hear it,' says Liv, coming in from the garden. She raises her eyebrows a little at the sight of the glass so early in the day and thinks that Em looks rather like Mo. 'We're going to need our pride with Rosie and Roop coming for the weekend. We need more than pride. We need a bloody miracle.'

'I think we've just had one,' says Em – and recounts the telephone call.

'Brilliant,' says Liv, her eyes beginning to shine. 'Bloody brilliant. Where are those sheets of sticky labels you bought for the jam. We'll grubby them up a bit and stick 'em all over the furniture.'

'Hang on,' says Em quickly, having another quick gulp at the gin. 'Hang on. Will they believe it's Mo's writing?'

'We'll print them,' says Liv triumphantly. 'Not too uniform. A bit wavery but not enough for Roop to say that Mo was potty when she wrote them. Come on, Em. We've got work to do.'

'It's terrible,' says Rosie, long-faced. 'Don't think I don't feel it too. I lived here all my life, remember, until I got married. It's so sad to see a home broken up. But we must try to be brave.' She gives a deep sigh. 'Now where shall we start?'

The girls have done very well but naturally they can't label everything and they agree that it would look suspicious if they were to do so. Luckily the things that are precious to them by association are also the things that are the most valuable. There are one or two smaller things that they hope to keep simply because Rosie and Roop won't want them.

'She's not having Mo's flask,' says Emmy firmly. 'It was Grandmother's to begin with. Then Pamela had it. Then Mo . . . Would *you* like it?'

Liv remarks a faintly wistful tone in Em's question and smiles. She suspects that the flask is already full and hopes that Em's recent Mo-like tendencies are merely a result of her meeting with the lawyer and will pass in due course.

'No, no,' she says. 'You keep it. As long as one of us has got it.'

'That's what I thought,' says Em, relieved, slipping it into her jacket pocket. 'We'll share.'

Now, Liv and Em stare at Rosie with open guileless faces.

'Where would you like to start?' asks Liv, almost indifferently. 'Shall we start in the drawing room? Perhaps you'd like the carpet? Oh and we mustn't forget the wallpaper.'

Roop is angry. Liv and Em are neither bowed down with grief nor subdued by humiliation. He has cornered them, yet they refuse to acknowledge it.

'You really haven't taken it in, have you?' he begins spitefully. 'You just haven't got any idea what's going on here.'

Rosie looks warningly at him and he subsides. Hands in pockets, face sullen, he watches from the sidelines.

'Well,' says Rosie, looking round and wondering how tactless it would be to start with Mo's bureau. She decides instead to start on some lesser, though very desirable object. 'What about the glass-fronted bookcase?' she suggests. 'We could just about squeeze it in, I suppose.'

'Squeeze it in to what?' asks Liv.

'Our drawing room,' says Rosie, patiently, 'if you can't bear the idea of it being sold. What do you think?'

'It's Liv's,' says Emmy, surprised. 'Why should *you* have it?'

'Nothing is *anybody's*,' cries Roop, unable to control himself. 'For God's *sake*, can't we get this clear?'

He glares at Rosie, furious and frustrated, but she glares back and he grits his teeth and balls his fists in his pockets.

'But surely we have to respect the wishes of the dead?' asks Emmy, as though genuinely seeking information. 'We were told that it was quite in order if the deceased person has left some kind of instruction.'

Rosie and Roop exchange an uneasy look.

'What kind of instruction?' asks Rosie attempting a lightness she does not feel. 'Just because Mo made some comment twenty years ago . . .'

'Oh, no,' protests Liv gently. 'Nothing so vague as that. You must remember that a lot of the things in this house came to Fa through *my* mother and to Mo through Em's father. Mo was always very firm that those pieces should belong to us when she and Fa were gone.'

Rosie looks stunned and Roop is white-faced. 'Wait,' he says. 'Hang on a minute. I want to know about these instructions.' He turns to Rosie. 'Do you know who the stuff belonged to?'

'No,' she says with angry reluctance. 'But we need proof.'

'We were told that what Mo did was more than adequate,' says Liv. 'She put labels on everything.'

'She did *what*?' cries Roop, beside himself. Rosie is silent.

'Look,' says Liv, smiling sweetly at him. 'See? It's just here.'

She swings open the door and Rosie and Roop crane to see the grubby sticker inscribed with '*For Livy. Her mother's bookcase.*'

Roop and Rosie stare at one another and then around the drawing room.

'It's not enough,' says Roop slowly. 'It would never stand up in court.'

'Oh, I think you're wrong, Roop,' says Emmy gently. 'We took advice. An old lawyer friend of mine came down to see us. He was very helpful. I'm sure you remember him, Rosie?' She laughs. 'Yes I see you do. He remembers you, too. We'll have a chat about it later. Meanwhile,' she looks about her, 'what shall we look at next?'

# 19

'They've stitched us up,' rages Roop. 'I just know it. I'm going to contest this.'

'Don't be silly,' mutters Rosie. 'I can just see us standing up in court and making a fuss because my two sisters want to keep some of their own furniture. For Christ's sake! How do you think it would look? Do you honestly think we'd get away with it? Don't you think they've taken advice?'

'What's all this about a lawyer?' asks Roop, momentarily distracted. 'What was all that about?'

Rosie thinks quickly. She and Roop are in their bedroom, regrouping after an abortive tour of the house. Most of the pieces of value are marked down to Liv and Em, although there are several things marked for Rosie: enough things to allay suspicion. Defeated, Roop and Rosie have retired to take stock.

'It's nothing,' says Rosie, opening the suitcase. 'Emmy had a boyfriend who was a lawyer, oh yonks ago. I was about . . . seventeen. She brought him home and he fell for me.' She shrugs. 'What was I supposed to do about it? It caused a lot of bad feeling and now and again she has a dig about it. It couldn't matter less.'

'It's obvious that they've taken advice from him, though,' says Roop. 'But I'm still going to check it out for myself.'

'You do that,' says Rosie. She has decided that it will be better if Roop is out of the way whilst she lays her plans. She doesn't want Emmy telling him the truth about the lawyer. 'Look,' she says, 'I'm not leaving this house until things are settled. You go back and get your developer friend going. I'm not waiting about any longer.'

'Good.' Roop stares at her. 'You look as if you've had an idea.'

'I have,' says Rosie. 'They can't stop us accepting a good offer for the house unless they decide they want to bring in their own valuer to hold things up. Either way, the house is going.'

'What about the furniture?' says Roop, his frustration returning.

Rosie smiles. 'Have you noticed,' she asks, 'how *big* the furniture is? Can you honestly see them cramming it all in to a flat or a cottage?'

'It'll still be theirs,' he says crossly.

'Mmm,' says Rosie reflectively, 'but they might get to a stage where they simply can't be bothered any more. Know what I mean?'

Roop is silent for a moment whilst hope springs eternal in his breast. 'I think I see what you're getting at,' he says softly. 'But they'll have enough between them to buy quite a reasonable house, you know. Bigish.'

'Only,' says Rosie firmly, 'if they leave no funds for investment. Trust me. We'll be OK but just leave it all to me now. You go back and get things moving. I'll phone you.'

In the kitchen Emmy and Liv are congratulating themselves. They laugh and laugh until the tears come.

'His *face*!' they moan to one another. 'Did you see his *face*!' At the remembrance of Roop's reaction at the label on each piece of furniture they go off into fresh paroxysms and, when Rosie and Roop suddenly appear at the kitchen door, they are barely able to contain their mirth.

'Roop's going off,' says Rosie stonily.

'He's been off for years,' mutters Em, who has resorted once or twice to the flask, and at this well-worn childish joke she and Liv collapse yet again.

'For God's sake,' says Roop, his temper rising – but Rosie nudges him quickly. She has no wish to precipitate some unpleasant truths and she sees that the girls are in exactly the right mood for telling the whole tale of that distant Boxing Day.

'Is it too much to ask,' she says, as if she is talking to two delinquents, 'to organise some lunch before he goes?'

Giggling, Emmy and Liv jostle in and out of the larder, laying lunch on the kitchen table and going off into fits of laughter each time they catch the other's eye.

'I'm so glad,' says Roop icily, 'that you can find something to laugh at.'

Yet again Rosie quells him with a look and he eats his lunch sullenly, burning with longings for revenge. He dwells on the sweet thought of the house being turned into flats; the vision of the shrubs and plants that Mo planted being ripped up to make walkways for the new owners. He has a delightful picture of Livy and Em driving away to some poky flat into which none of their precious belongings will fit. He has every intention of being there on that day, waving them down the drive.

When he has gone, Rosie takes herself off for a walk to think things through while the girls wash up and clear away. They have been sobered by the information that Rosie will be staying with them for much longer than a weekend; 'for as long as it takes,' she says, 'to sort everything out.' At this ominous phrase their euphoria dissipates and they remember that, although they may have won a battle, they will certainly lose the war.

'I'd forgotten it in all the excitement,' says Emmy forlornly. 'What's the point of keeping the furniture if we haven't got anywhere to put it?'

'We shall have somewhere to put it,' answers Liv. 'But that's not the point. We want it here, in this house.'

'It's not just bloody mindedness,' says Em, throwing down the dishcloth and collapsing at the table. 'I just can't stand the thought of going. I can't bear to think that I shan't be able to go out on the first warm day of spring and see the snowdrops in the corner by the wall. Or the daffodils on the bank by the summerhouse.'

'We always celebrate when the house martins come,' says Liv, joining her at the table. 'Was it Pamela who started that?'

'Well, Mo always used to get very excited about them. She used to rush in and tell everyone. It was Pamela who decided that we ought to celebrate with a drink.'

Liv laughs sadly. 'That figures,' she says.

'There are so many things,' says Em sighing. 'Things that mark the arrival of the seasons and the passing of the year. Things that were here when I was born and things that Mo and Fa did later.'

They stare at one another across the table.

'I can't take it in,' says Em. 'I simply can't believe that this can happen. And for what? So that Rosie and Roop can have more money. They've got the London house and the cottage. Roop has an enormous salary and a good pension. Why?'

'Because they're greedy,' says Liv. 'They've always been the same. They get each other going. And they hate us. That business with the furniture was the last straw. Did you see Roop's face at lunch? God, how he hates us!'

They sit unhappily at the table; all desire to laugh has long since left them. Emmy feels in her pocket for the flask.

'Let's have a drink,' she says.

*   *   *

Rosie sees the fight ebbing out of them and feels triumphant. As the days pass and she sees the hopelessness on their faces she knows that she will probably be able to win back some of the furniture. She suspects that in the end they won't care one way or the other. Systematically, Rosie does what has to be done; contacting the executor; arranging for several local estate agents to value the house so that she can show more than one estimate. She knows that Roop's man will top them all. Roop and the developer come down for a flying visit and Roop rejoices openly when he sees Em's and Livy's expressions as they hear what is to be done. He makes quite certain that they realise exactly what is to be pulled down, ripped out, concreted over. He returns to London delighted.

By the end of ten days, Rosie is hardly bothering to talk to the girls. They wander about in a daze as their world crumbles rapidly about them. Em takes refuge in the contents of the flask and even Liv is drinking more than usual.

'I wish I'd killed her,' says Em, as she and Liv sit in the summerhouse, staring out. 'I wish I'd killed her that day on the terrace.'

Once again she feels the berry in her fingers, sees it sliding out of Rosie's dribbling mouth.

'So do I,' mutters Liv, teeth clenched. 'Bloody Boswell.'

She remembers how he struggled; the feel of his fur and his sinews straining under her hands.

'So *there* you are.' Rosie stands before them, not bothering to hide her triumphant smile. 'You know, you really don't have time to sit idling in the sun. You should be out house-hunting, doing something constructive. Have you looked at those details I got for you? A nice little cottage in the town. Of course, you'd never get all that furniture in.' She is laughing openly now. 'Oh well. It's up to you.

Don't forget that Roop is coming to pick me up later.' She
shakes her head at their silence, raises her eyebrows, shrugs.
'Well, don't blame me if you finish up homeless.'

She walks away, still laughing at the little sting in the last
remark. Emmy and Liv sit on.

'God, I hate her,' says Liv, conversationally. 'Bloody
Boswell.'

Emmy remembers the berry in her fingers, the deadly
nightshade growing in the wood.

'Perhaps,' she says slowly, 'perhaps we ought to give
it another try. The deadly nightshade still grows in the
wood.'

Liv snorts, amused. 'Make her a nice fruits of the forest
gâteau?' she suggests.

'Mince pies,' says Emmy thoughtfully. 'She's always liked
my mince pies.'

Liv looks at her sharply. Em is not joking. 'But . . . But
we'd be found out. Most people don't put deadly nightshade in their mince pies. If you die suddenly they do an
autopsy.'

'Who cares?' asks Emmy dully, thinking about her lawyer
and all that she has lost. 'What could they do to me?'

Liv is still pondering ways and means as a kind of intellec-
tual exercise. 'Perhaps we could say that we were momentarily unhinged by the thought of losing our home?'

They sit together, brooding.

'We'd probably get off,' says Em at last. 'I've got some
pastry in the fridge. Just time to make some pies for lunch.'

Liv glances at her watch. 'Shit!' she says. 'Got to dash
down to the village or there won't *be* any lunch.' She pats
Em's arm. 'Never mind. Nice thought. See you later.'

Em takes another pull at the flask. She watches a robin
in the hedge and thinks of all the years the robin's family
has been fed through the winter. Who will feed the robin
now? The thought is too much for her to bear. Rage,

misery, despair surge through her and she gets up, rather unsteadily, and crosses the lawn, making for the little gate which leads into the wood . . . The deadly nightshade is tall and succulent, bursting with life. Em hears Miss Taylor's voice: '*Each part of the plant is poisonous.*' Slowly Em reaches forward and begins to pick the berries.

Before Liv gets back from the village, the pies are made and in the oven and Em is fiddling about in the larder, humming to herself. She has taken six mince pies out of the freezer and has come across one or two bags, the contents of which she feels it might be prudent to throw away. One of these bags contains half a dozen small and very old meat pies which she feels are well past their sell-by date and she takes them into the kitchen and crushes them down on top of the rubbish in the bin. Still humming, she takes the deadly little pies from the oven and arranges them on a pretty flowered plate. Each pie is marked with a cross. On a nearby identical plate, the six mince pies from the freezer have been defrosting, and now she slips them into the oven to warm them through.

When Liv comes into the kitchen the two plates stand side by side and Emmy, looking rather flushed, giggles, covering her mouth with her hand.

'*Don't* eat the ones with the cross,' she says; laughter escapes in little spurts and her eyes are bright and slightly mad. '*Those* are for Rosie. *These* are OK. I've sugared them.'

Livy stares at her, puzzled. 'What are you talking about?'

'The pies,' whispers Em. 'You know . . . ?'

Liv is frightened now. 'What have you done?' she whispers. 'You haven't actually *cooked* some poisoned pies . . . Oh, God, you have. Which are they? *Em!*' She shakes her urgently by the arm. '*Which?*'

'The ones with the cross.' Em hiccups. 'Whoops. Don't eat them. They're for darling Rosie. The Little Princess.'

Liv picks up the plate but, as she does so, Rosie comes into the kitchen behind her.

'Is lunch ready?' she asks. 'I did say I'd need an early one.'

Livy has slipped into the larder, pushed the plate of pies to the back of a shelf and now emerges carrying a loaf.

'Nearly there,' she says. 'I've just been down to the village and bought some ham and tomatoes. Soup's on the stove.'

Em watches her. Livy's sudden action has sobered her a little and she sits down at the table feeling oddly faint and confused. Liv puts a bowl of soup before her and presently, as lunch proceeds, she begins to recover. Rosie makes a good meal and eats two pies. Liv watches her, praying that Em has not got her plates muddled. She glances at Em, who is looking more normal now. The mad look is gone and she is very quiet. Liv deliberately directs her eyes towards the pies and then raises her eyebrows. Emmy shakes her head, looking pale. It has just dawned upon her what she intended to do and she feels shaky and frightened. To set Liv's mind at rest, she reaches forward and takes a pie. Liv draws a deep breath and gets up to make coffee; she pours Em's strong and black.

As they are finishing, Roop is heard arriving and Rosie dashes away to finish packing. Livy goes after her. Em is suddenly sober enough to be determined that she will not feed Roop and she packs the ham and cheese away into the fridge, putting the three mince pies into a bag and popping them back in the freezer.

'Too late,' she says to Roop as he puts his head round the kitchen door. 'We've finished. What a pity.'

She passes him in the doorway and goes upstairs, feeling a desperate need to lie down. Roop glares after her but goes into the kitchen anyway and snoops about. He pinches a slice of ham from the fridge and then sees the plate of pies on the shelf, half hidden under some bags. He laughs to himself, guessing that Emmy has put them there so that he shouldn't see them. Roop likes his pies sugared and he takes down the bag of caster sugar from the shelf and covers them generously. He gulps one down quickly . . . and then another, one ear cocked. He has decided that he will leave the rest on the kitchen table so that Emmy will see that she has been thwarted. He eats a third and, hearing Rosie's voice raised impatiently, he closes the larder door behind him, puts the plate down on the kitchen table and hurries out.

Coming back to do the washing up, Livy sees the pies still on the table and imagines they are the leftovers from lunch. She puts them in a bag and pops them into the freezer. She notices that the plate of pies is no longer on the larder shelf and hurries to the waste bin. There is a bag of pies squashed on the top of the rubbish, their crusts broken, and she heaves a sigh of relief. At least Emmy is in her right mind again.

'Sorry,' says Em later, when she comes downstairs after a heavy sleep. 'I can't think what came over me. I think I was a bit tipsy. I felt most peculiar. I can't quite remember what I did with them . . .'

'It's OK,' says Liv. 'All dealt with. Let's forget it.'

'Sorry,' says Em again, shamefaced.

Liv laughs. 'I wish I'd had the courage to let you go through with it,' she says.

As he turns onto the motorway, Roop begins to feel unwell. His eyes won't focus properly and his heart jumps most alarmingly; his throat is dry and he feels hot. He is just about to suggest that they stop as soon as possible so that Rosie can drive, when he has a knife-like pain in his gut. A second, more violent, pain causes him to arch backwards, thrusting his foot down sharply on the accelerator. The car cuts across the bend, crashes through the barrier and topples down the bank to the field below. It lands upside down, rocks for a moment . . . and then bursts into a tall column of flame.

# 20 ∫

It is several days before the news of the accident trickles back to the girls. They are coming to terms with the fact that they must leave and have been looking half-heartedly at the details from estate agents which Rosie has made certain that they will receive. They shuffle the papers to and fro across the kitchen table, reading out the descriptions and staring at the photographs.

'I don't like any of them,' says Liv, propping her chin in her hands. 'Perhaps we should go right away. Somewhere completely different. Cornwall. Or Scotland.'

'I don't think,' says Emmy, 'that I could bear to live near enough to see what is going to happen. Did you hear that ghastly man tell Roop that he would grub up all the rhododendrons?'

'And even if we don't come and look,' says Liv grimly, 'there will be hundreds of people who will want to tell us about it. I should have let you give Rosie those mince pies.'

'I still feel ill when I think about it,' admits Emmy. 'I must have been mad. I wouldn't have stood a chance.'

'And it would still have left Roop,' points out Liv. 'We need a miracle that disposes of both of them. My God! you gave me a fright, though.'

Emmy begins to laugh. She is still shocked at what she did and has vowed to cut down a little on the gin. 'I was out of my head,' she says, chuckling. 'Away with the fairies. It seemed quite reasonable to me at the time.'

'Oh, it was perfectly *reasonable*,' says Liv. 'It was a great idea in theory. I just didn't want us to spend the rest of our lives in Broadmoor.'

'It didn't seem to matter at the time,' says Em sadly. 'I'm not sure it does now. Not if I've got to leave here.'

'Well, it's too late to hope for miracles,' sighs Liv. 'But I think we should consider making a completely new start . . . Oh shit! Who's that?'

'God knows!' Em stands up and goes out to the hall.

Liv sits riffling idly through the house details, one ear cocked towards the hall. She can hear a deep voice talking monotonously, then a low stifled cry from Emmy. Pushing back her chair, Liv hurries into the hall. Standing with Em is a police constable. He is holding her arm as though he is supporting her and he looks with relief towards Livy.

'What is it?' she asks. For a mad moment she thinks that Em is being arrested and she seizes Em's other arm protectively. 'What's going on?'

Emmy turns to look at her, the most peculiar expression on her face. It is compounded of shock and suppressed excitement and she tries to send a warning with her eyes.

'The most terrible news,' she says in a shaky voice, her eyes still warning Liv to react cautiously. 'It's dreadful. Rosie and Roop have been killed in a car accident.'

Liv is so shocked that she actually staggers and the police constable leaps to help her. '*Killed*?'

'Their car went off the road, madam. They couldn't have known a thing about it,' explains the young constable who has already related this to Emmy. He wishes they could go to some room where these two old biddies could sit down. He doesn't want them passing out on him. 'Perhaps we should go into the kitchen?' he suggests hopefully. 'I could make you some tea.'

'Went off the road? But how?' demands Liv eagerly, as the three of them totter kitchenwards. Emmy gives her arm a little pinch. 'I can't believe it,' says Liv, hastily responding by dropping her voice to a grieving kind of sadness.

'They wouldn't have suffered,' says the constable reassuringly. 'The car just shot off the road and burst into flames. The driver of the car following said it was over in seconds. They think the driver had a heart attack. That was your brother-in-law?' Now that they are seated safely at the table he is able to pull out his notebook. 'Rupert Cartwright?'

'That's quite right,' agrees Emmy who has adopted a sorrowing mien. 'Of course, Rosie was our *step*-sister, you know.' She adds this lest the constable feels that neither she nor Liv is displaying the proper degree of grief. 'We saw them very rarely.'

The constable, relieved that he won't have to cope with hysterics, consults his notebook again and gives the place, date and time of the accident. 'Had they been visiting?' he asks. 'The accident took place less than twenty miles away.'

The girls explain that this was indeed the case. They had been discussing whether the house should be sold now that their mother was dead; Rupert and Rosie had come down to give advice.

'I see,' says the constable. 'Was your brother-in-law subject to heart problems?'

There is a long pause.

'Roop – ert,' says Liv carefully but rather sadly, 'was very overweight. He over-indulged, shall we say? But we know very little really. As we've told you, we rarely saw them.'

'He looked unhealthy,' puts in Em helpfully. 'Very poor colour. Will there be some kind of –' she shudders artistically – 'autopsy, do you call it? Post mortem?'

The young constable looks distressed. 'The car blew up,' he explains. How is it possible to deal sensitively with these things? 'I'm afraid any kind of – uh, you know –

examination is out of the question. The coroner's court will deal with it.'

Liv stares at the tablecloth. Em reaches for her handkerchief. The constable watches them anxiously.

'I'm sure you know,' he says tentatively, 'that there is a helpline should you require counselling. Perhaps you would like the number?'

Liv looks at Em, poker-faced. Emmy stares back.

'I think that's a very good idea,' she says with just a hint of a break in her voice. 'Speaking for myself, I know that I just haven't taken it in. It's too . . . too . . .' She shakes her head and bites her lip.

'Exactly,' says Liv. 'I feel just the same. Perhaps we ought to have that number.'

The constable gives them the leaflet. He tells them that a form will be put through the door of the house in Chelsea so that when Alice returns she will be able to contact the police for details but he explains that it is up to Emmy and Liv to contact any other relatives. He offers to make tea, asks a few more questions and prepares to leave. They see him out and watch him down the drive before returning to the kitchen in silence. They sit down and stare at each other across the table.

'*Dead?*' whispers Emmy. '*Both dead?*'

Liv shakes her head, marvelling. 'And I said it was too late for a miracle,' she says.

'Honestly,' says Emmy with a convulsive but guilty giggle. 'Honestly, Liv. It's terrible really.'

'No it isn't!' says Liv strongly. 'Don't be such a hypocrite. Holy shit, Em! You were planning to *poison* her two days ago.'

'I know,' says Em, 'I know. But still . . .'

'Em.' Liv leans across the table and grasps Emmy's wrist. 'It's done with. Over. They're gone. Don't you see? We can *stay* here.'

Joy bursts over Em's face and she presses her lips together as if she must hold it in. 'Oh, Liv,' she says, 'I know. And just think. We might have ended up in Broadmoor.'

They begin to laugh; silent, wicked, hysterical laughter. They rock to and fro and then get up and dance around the kitchen. Freeman, Hardy and Willis are offended by such behaviour and withdraw to the breakfast room.

'A drink,' gasps Liv. 'I need a drink.'

Em fishes out her flask and offers Liv a pull. She watches her, laughing at Liv's antics.

'Don't you feel the least bit sorry?' she asks. 'That policeman must have thought we were hard as nails.'

'Look,' says Liv, suddenly sober, 'they would have taken everything we had. Our home and our belongings. And the more we loved those things, the more they would have enjoyed depriving us. Didn't you see Roop's face when he brought down that ghastly little man? Didn't you see him watching us as he explained how the house would be gutted and Mo's roses destroyed and Fa's summerhouse pulled down and burned? I watched him watching us and at that moment I felt that boiling in oil was too good for him.' She smiles bitterly at Em. 'Too late now for regret. He was a bastard and so was Rosie. They'd have put Mo in a home if they could have wrung a few pennies out of it. They'd have seen us in the gutter and laughed. Come on. We'll drink a toast to them. A farewell.' She raises the flask. 'To Rosie and Roop. Wherever you are, I hope you bloody fry!'

Alice is still unaware of the death of her parents. She has left no forwarding address and she sees none of the advertisements which Roop's lawyer puts in the newspapers. She moves about a great deal. There are several unsavoury acquaintances who would give a great deal to know where Alice is; people to whom she has lied; people she has cheated and double-crossed; people to whom she has introduced the drug on which they now depend and for which, in their turn, they will cheat and lie – and even kill.

Back in England, Roop's developer is trying to contact her. Knowing that she is the beneficiary, he is hoping that she will pick up where Roop left off. He outlines the scheme and points out the advantages. The letter lies with the others on the mat in the house in Chelsea.

Emmy and Liv are enjoying to the full the feeling of security. Husbanding their resources carefully, they begin to restore the house and garden. Emmy resumes the decoration of the drawing room and Livy works in the garden during the bright autumn days. They make plans and decide that, if it comes to it, they might sell one or two of the pieces which are valuable but not particularly precious to them.

'We'll hang on as long as we can,' says Liv. 'We don't need anything fancy. It's amazing what a few pots of paint can achieve.'

'We'll be drawing the old age pension in three years' time,' says Emmy. 'Can you believe it?'

'It's getting through the winter that worries me,' says Liv. 'We must keep warm.'

'We'll take the cats to bed with us,' smiles Emmy. 'Like Pamela did. You know, I still really miss Pamela and Mo.'

'So do I,' admits Liv. 'Oh, Em. Thank God, we didn't have to leave.'

'It's lovely,' says Em, 'to have the time to do things. Next spring I'm going to move that summerhouse.'

'I still think that it won't survive it,' says Liv stubbornly. 'It's nearly fifty years since Fa built it and we've never looked after it properly.'

'Then we'll buy a new one and leave Fa's where it is,' says Em cheerfully. 'We'll have to do the Lottery.'

'Well that gives us a one in fifty-seven million chance,' says Liv. 'Of course, we could give up booze and save the money.' Emmy looks at her, shocked, and Liv nods, resigned. 'You're right. We've got more chance of winning the Lottery.'

A few days later, a woman comes toiling up the drive from the village. She is Jackie, Betty's daughter. Betty has died and Jackie and her husband, Joe, having inherited the little cottage in the village, have moved back from London. Jackie is coming to pay her respects. She was very fond of Mo, who gave her sweeties when she was small, and she wonders if Emmy and Liv would like a hand in the house. Joe has been made redundant and she is hoping that there may be work for him in the garden. As Jackie crosses the gravel she gives a gasp of fright. Away across the lawn, near the old summerhouse, Mo and Pamela are walking together. She remembers Pamela, the eccentric American relation who lived with Mo, but she knows that she is dead: that they are both dead.

Standing still, her heart pounding madly, Jackie watches the two ghosts. Pamela looks like an old grey wolf, long-stepping, lean and prowling; Mo, at her side, looks like a small grey mouse scurrying along. Jackie even thinks that she recognises the clothes. She does. Wearing Pamela's and Mo's old clothes are part of Emmy's and Liv's economies. As they approach her, they wave to her, calling out to her.

'We thought it was you,' cries Emmy-Mo. 'To begin with we thought it was Betty but then we realised . . .'

'We thought we were seeing a ghost,' agrees Livy-Pamela. 'You *did* give us a turn.'

'Yes,' gasps Jackie-Betty, weak with relief now that she realises her mistake. 'I know just what you mean. How are you both? I was so sorry to hear about your mum.'

'And we're so sorry about Betty,' says Emmy, hugging her warmly. 'Come on in and have some tea and we'll catch up on the news.'

As she follows them inside she sees the signs of poverty and her heart bleeds for them. She abandons her idea of asking for work but intends to help them if she can. They smile upon her but look anxious when the subject of biscuits with her tea arises. She assures them that she never eats biscuits and they look relieved. Her heart is touched further and an idea occurs to her. Later, after several cups of tea, she broaches it.

'It's about that old kitchen garden,' she says. 'I don't suppose you grow much there these days?'

'It's gone to seed a bit,' admits Liv. 'I've kept a few things going but it's a shocking mess. It's too big for me.'

'It's Joe,' says Jackie. 'He's missing his allotment something awful. And Mum's cottage hasn't got hardly enough to grow a lettuce. Supposing he was to come up here a few hours a week? There'd be vegetables enough for us all.'

Liv and Emmy exchange an embarrassed glance.

'It would be lovely,' says Em, 'but you see, we couldn't afford to pay him anything.'

'No, no,' says Jackie quickly, as embarrassed as they are. 'He wouldn't want paying. He just needs the land, see? You'd get free vegetables in exchange.'

'But that would be wonderful,' cries Liv. 'I could give him a hand. We'd really enjoy fresh vegetables, wouldn't we Em?'

'We certainly would,' says Em gratefully. 'It's a brilliant idea, Jackie. You must bring Joe up to meet us.'

Jackie hurries away feeling oddly happy. It's as if Mo and Pamela are still alive and she has a sense of continuity. It's good to be back in the village, back in the country, and she laughs as she hurries down the lane thinking of how she thought Emmy and Liv were ghosts. Joe will enjoy the joke.

# 21 ∫

Emmy and Liv are very happy through the winter. Just as Betty worked for Mo and Pamela long after they could afford to pay her properly, so Jackie helps Livy and Em. When it seems that she is going to keep popping up to check on them and lend a hand, they insist that she must have some sort of payment; part cash, part in goods. Joe borrows tools to use in his own house and garden and Jackie trundles home with a pile of nearly new curtains unearthed in the attic. When she sees the quantities of stuff crammed into the two huge rooms under the roof, her eyes stretch.

'What you should do,' she tells them, 'is to sort it out and take it to a car boot sale. You'd do really well.'

The girls are interested by this idea and it is agreed that, with Joe and Jackie to keep an eye on them, they will go along to the next sale and see how much they can earn. They do very well indeed and enjoy it enormously. They insist that their two helpers take a commission and they begin to plan for the next sale. Joe watches over them like a guard dog.

'Trouble is,' he tells Jackie, 'it's like they're not in this world. They haven't got a clue really. It's frightening.'

'It's having been stuck up here all those years on their own looking after their mum and that old aunt,' explains

Jackie defensively. She won't hear a word against them. 'They've been cut off. They're living twenty years back.'

'And those clothes,' says Joe, grinning a little.

'They can't afford new clothes,' says Jackie sharply. 'Those old things are good quality. That's something.'

Joe rather enjoys the look on the punters' faces when Emmy and Liv start bartering. 'They may be behind the times but they certainly drive a hard bargain,' he says admiringly.

Joe hires a chain saw and cuts up some old trees that have fallen in the orchard and at the edge of the wood. It looks as if Emmy and Mo might keep warm through the winter after all. They insist that he takes some wood for himself but the small cottage is centrally heated and he and Jackie don't bother too much to light a fire in the little grate in the living room. He takes a couple of bags for special occasions, like Christmas Day, and stacks the rest in the girls' empty woodshed. Emmy and Liv take plastic bags and go into the wood to collect twigs and fallen branches for kindling. Joe, following them, sees that there is plenty of larger stuff here that can be dragged back and sawn up and soon the woodshed begins to look satisfyingly full.

Before many weeks have passed, the house and garden are looking cared for again and, with the proceeds from the car boot sales, Liv and Emmy are able to plan for the new summerhouse. Joe will lay a skim of concrete over the yard and the old well and then assemble the summerhouse on the top of it. Liv and Emmy spend hours choosing the design from the glossy catalogues.

'We'll have a verandah this time,' says Em.

'And plenty of windows,' adds Liv. 'So we get all the sun.'

They can hardly wait for the spring to come, and to pass the time they sort through the attics and prepare for the next car boot sale.

\*     \*     \*

Meanwhile, Alice is learning that greed and low cunning are not quite enough when it comes to making a fortune and that she is moving in a world where she has much to learn. She makes one or two very serious and costly mistakes and has to lie low. During the winter she becomes ill; she needs her regular supply of heroin and her funds become seriously depleted. As spring approaches she knows that it is time to visit England and blackmail Rosie out of some more money.

Locally, Emmy and Liv are beginning to acquire a kind of charisma. A great deal of this is due to Jackie and Joe who talk about them in the pub. Gradually the old stories of the 'coven' and Mo's disastrous visit to the Good Samaritan, not to mention Liv's ill-fated romance with the doctor, all begin to become the stuff of legend. Memories of Pamela struggling home with a full and clinking basket are recalled with sympathetic laughter. 'She was a great old girl,' someone says reminiscently into his beer. 'Don't make 'em like that any more,' says another, shaking his head. Joe, who secretly disposes of a surprisingly large quantity of bottles at the bottle-bank in the car park in the town, stays silent. He knows that Livy and Em are chips off the old blocks.

When they start turning up at the car boot sales, hopping out of the car, laying out their goodies and enjoying the good tempered banter, their stock rises even higher. They are no longer ignored when they come down to do their shopping and Em even pops into the pub with Joe for a quick one. She is perfectly happy to josh with the barmaid, reminding her that they were at the village school together and chuckling with her over the idiosyncrasies of the long-dead headmistress.

'After all,' says the barmaid as she wipes down the bar

with reflective sweeps of the cloth. 'She's one of us, isn't she? Her family have been up on the hill for hundreds of years.'

When Pamela takes an ailing Freeman – or Hardy – or Willis down to the vet's weekly surgery, she encounters an elderly lady who remembers Pamela buying the kittens. 'She stopped at the shop to get extra milk,' she says, smiling at the memory, 'and brought them in to show us. We *did* laugh when she told us what she was going to call them.'

The fact that, at the time, Pamela was referred to as 'mad as a bloody hatter' and a bystander affected surprise that the kittens wouldn't be brought up on gin, has been forgotten. The waiting room laughs at the story and hopes that Freeman – or Hardy – or Willis will recover.

Thus Livy and Em are accepted back into the community.

So the winter passes. At Christmas, Liv receives a card from the doctor wishing her well and telling her that he still thinks of her. Emmy has written to her lawyer at his office, telling him of Roop's and Rosie's deaths and explaining that she and Liv are now quite safe. Since he knows nothing of Alice's existence, and Emmy doesn't mention her, he doesn't warn the girls that they are not safe at all. He has decided that it is wisest to have as little contact as possible but he too sends a card at Christmas and the girls feel happy to be remembered. Their bitterness has abated a little and they concentrate on making the house as cosy as possible and keeping themselves busy.

Despite Joe's help with the logs, they are very glad when signs of spring arrive. The house is too big to heat and they tend to live in the breakfast room and the kitchen by day and pack themselves about with hot-water bottles by night, sharing out the cats between them. As February draws on and there are one or two days of warm gentle weather, they heave sighs of relief. The worst is over.

Emmy wanders in the garden, noting the first snowdrops beneath the sheltering wall and the green spikes of the daffodils which will blow upon the grassy bank in March. The birds, which she has fed all winter, are loudly proclaiming their territories and the robin watches her, head cocked, hoping for crumbs. She opens up the summerhouse and sits for a moment in the sunshine, remembering how she has sat there on other occasions. She thinks of Fa's pride when it was first erected and how Grandmother was ushered out to give it her seal of approval and how they had tea to celebrate. She thinks of Pamela and Mo, relaxing here in the sun, and how she and Liv sat in these basket chairs and talked about poisoning Rosie.

It still comes as a little shock as she recalls how she went into the wood and picked the berries of the deadly nightshade. The whole affair is hazy but she shudders when she thinks that she might be languishing in a prison cell rather than sitting here in the sun.

'I thought you'd be here,' says Liv, who has appeared beside her. 'Glorious morning. Pity about the motorway. Oh, I know it will be different when we build the new summerhouse.'

'The road will be hidden,' points out Emmy, 'and we shall look across to the hills. If we site the summerhouse carefully we shan't see the road at all.'

'We shall still be able to hear it though,' argues Livy. 'And don't go on about it sounding like the sea. I *know* it's a motorway. It doesn't sound a bit like the sea.'

'Anyway,' says Emmy, resorting to their private joke, 'it's better than Broadmoor.'

Alice returns to England in April. It is in her nature to travel cautiously, to hide and watch, and she warns no one of her visit. She likes to take people by surprise. So she comes secretly, hitching a lift by night with a colleague who owns a boat which plies regularly between the French and English coasts, carrying drugs. They motor into Chichester Harbour in the early hours of the morning, whilst it is growing light, passing between the moorings, heading up river towards West Wittering, where it is easy to drop the anchor and row a passenger quietly ashore. The packages are carried to a waiting car and Alice is driven away through back lanes and so to London.

She lets herself into the house and stares in surprise at the amount of post on the floor. She stands quite still, listening, looking about, and then bends to pick up some of the letters. Her own name on an envelope catches her eye and frowning a little she tears it open. It is the most recent letter from the now desperate developer. It begins quite baldly:

> *Dear Alice*
> *It is now nearly six months since your parents died and I am no longer prepared to keep my offer open to you. Various other propositions have come to my attention and, unless I hear from you within two weeks, my offer will be withdrawn . . .*

Alice looks quickly at the date at the top of the page, reads the letter through again and then searches through the envelopes on the floor for other communications from the developer . . . It is an excellent deal and she has three days in which to come to a decision. Typically, she does not telephone him but decides to travel down to the house and see how the land lies first. She is unmoved by the news of her parents' death. She realises that they are much more valuable to her dead than alive, nevertheless she sees no good reason for turning down an excellent deal simply because there will be other monies due to her in due course.

The developer is obviously very keen and might be good for an upfront sum in cash if she plays her cards right.

Alice tucks his letters into her bag so as to be able to peruse them at her leisure, lets herself out of the house and disappears into the morning rush hour. She visits a friend for whom she has a very precious package and later persuades him to drive her out into the country. She is dropped, at her own request, some distance from the house.

Unobserved she slips across the fields, close to the hedges, until she finds herself in the woods where she can see the house and part of the grounds. Hidden in thick bushes, she watches Joe working in the kitchen garden and sees Emmy and Liv on the lawn. It is several years since she has seen them and she too has a certain *frisson* at the sight of them together, looking so much like Pamela and Mo. She waits until Joe has packed up his tools and disappeared before she makes a move. Skirting the garden carefully, she slides into the old summerhouse, watching through the windows for signs of life.

She sees the gardener going off down the drive, perhaps he has been having a cup of tea, and, presently, Liv can be seen taking washing off the line which is strung across the little square of grass outside the back door. Emmy comes round to the front of the house and potters; collecting a trowel from a border and snipping a few dead heads with the secateurs. Liv leaves the washing basket at the back door and joins Emmy for a moment . . . As the dusk gathers, so at last is the garden deserted.

Alice leaves the summerhouse and moves carefully towards the back door. She stands beneath the lilac tree and watches Livy and Em in the lighted kitchen. She is able to hear the murmur of their voices but not the actual words. They are preparing supper, moving slowly, stopping to debate, pouring drinks. A cat leaps on to the window sill and stares out. Alice moves from the tree's shadow and crosses to the back door. She slips noiselessly in, creeps along the passage and pauses by the kitchen door to listen.

'. . . so he's coming on Thursday to lay the concrete,' Liv is saying. 'He and Jackie are off tomorrow to see his mum.'

'We'll have a party,' says Em. She sounds excited and happy. 'A summerhouse warming party.'

'Good idea,' says Liv. 'We'll drink to it. Perhaps we should wait until summer. What about Midsummer's Eve? The garden will be looking really good by then. We'll have a celebration.'

'What a *pity*,' says Em, laughing mockingly, 'that Rosie and Roop can't be here to see it.'

Exactly on cue, Alice opens the door. 'So it is,' she says, smiling widely at her aunts. 'A great pity. Never mind. Perhaps I'll make an adequate substitute?'

# 22 $\int$

To begin with, Emmy and Liv are surprised but not afraid. It is like Alice, somehow, to appear from nowhere and to refuse to give any explanation. She obviously knows about Rosie and Roop but seems to have no desire to discuss the accident to which the developer has referred at length in his earlier letters before his sympathy was replaced by impatience. They are shocked by her appearance; she is thin, no bigger than a child, and she looks much older than her years. Em's first thought is food. She and Livy live so frugally that there is rarely any spare food to be had. Her mind ranges anxiously about, relieved that their soup and cheese supper will obligingly stretch three ways.

Presently Alice goes upstairs with Livy to see about clean bedding and to have a wash before supper and Em roots about in the muddle of the freezer in the hope of discovering something filling. She fishes out a quiche and two halves of a sponge which can be filled with jam. As Em pushes aside the bags of frozen rhubarb and gooseberries, her fingers touch a smaller bag which feels more promising. She draws it out and sees that there are three mince pies inside liberally covered with sugar which has dropped into the corner of the bag. She places her findings on a rack on the larder shelf and, leaving them to thaw out, goes back to finish preparing supper.

There is something about Alice's presence which unsettles her and she pours herself another drink, topping up Livy's glass in her absence. She smiles a little to herself, remembering how Pamela used to call the buying of booze and ciggies 'Serious Shopping'. How right she was! thinks Emmy, as she puts away Livy's and her own soup bowl and brings out three smaller ones. She cuts the bread thinly and eyes the cheese, hoping that it will be enough.

Supper is a pleasant enough meal, although considering that Alice lives abroad she has little enough to say about it, but Livy and Em keep the conversation going. As the evening wears on, several more glasses of wine give Livy the courage to ask the question that has nagged at her for so long. She wants to be absolutely certain about the anonymous telephone call, just as Emmy is now certain as to what happened between her lawyer and Rosie on Boxing Day.

'Tell me,' she says, as Emmy makes coffee, 'was it you who told Rosie that I had an abortion?'

There is a moment of utter silence; Emmy freezes into immobility, a spoonful of coffee poised mid-air; Alice sits quite still, staring at her plate.

'Why yes,' she says at last, lifting her eyes and looking at Livy. 'Yes, it was me. I mentioned it in passing. Why?' Her smile is knowing and a little cruel. 'Was it a secret?'

Livy is silent. Emmy passes round mugs of coffee but the atmosphere has subtly changed. It is as if all three know that supper has merely been a prelude for something much more serious. Emmy's uneasy feeling is back and she looks at Liv who is gazing unsmilingly at nothing. Alice's lips curve upwards as her glance travels between the two of them. She knows the moment has come and pushing back her chair a little, one ankle cocked on a denim-clad knee, she begins to talk . . .

\*　　\*　　\*

At first, Livy and Em simply cannot believe it. By the time Alice has finished, however, they know that it is the truth; that they are back to the terrible position they were in nearly a year before. When Alice has made quite clear to them what she intends to do, she goes up to bed. She has been awake for nearly thirty-six hours and she is exhausted. She also needs a fix.

'It's too much,' says Emmy, grey-faced. 'Oh, I simply can't believe that this can be happening again.'

'We should have guessed,' says Liv grimly. 'What fools we've been. We should have known that Alice would inherit Rosie's share in the house.'

'It never occurred to me,' cries Em. 'She's our niece, not our sister.'

'It makes no difference,' says Liv. She wants to weep and scream and break things. 'After all we've done. I can't bear it.'

'But it's not fair,' says Emmy, tremblingly. 'She's got the house in London and the cottage . . .'

'She's Roop's daughter,' says Liv. 'She's greedy. She's got his eyes, have you noticed? She wants the lot. And she's got Rosie's ruthlessness to go with it. We haven't got a chance.'

They sit on, drinking and talking until, exhausted at last, they drag themselves up to bed. Their unsteady footsteps, their voices whispering on the landing, wake Alice who lies staring into the darkness. She feels ill; empty and sick with strange pains in her stomach. She decides that she's hungry and reluctantly she hauls herself out of bed and creeps downstairs in the dark. In the kitchen she roots about for biscuits but the tin is empty. She goes into the larder and opens the fridge which is disappointingly empty. She knows there is no cheese – she finished the last piece herself – but she remembers that there was a heel of bread left. She finds it in the crock and takes it back into the kitchen where she smothers it with butter and sits down to gnaw it. Her thoughts are busy with calculations and she feels pleased with her evening's work. Tomorrow – today rather – she will contact the developer and tell him what she proposes; no up-front cash, no deal.

Alice finishes her bread and realises that she still has an empty, faint feeling. She goes back into the larder and looks along the shelves. The quiche is thawing on the rack with the sponge but she spots the three little pies which are now quite ready to eat. She fetches a plate from the dresser, intending to carry the pies upstairs so as to eat them in bed. The kitchen is cold and she is feeling very shivery; her head swims and her body aches. She climbs the stairs quietly, shuts her bedroom door carefully behind her and slides back into bed. Resting back against her pillows, she begins to eat her pies . . .

Livy and Em wake to a sense of desolation; all their dreams have been dashed. How, they wonder, can they face the thought of dispossession for a second time? They look at each other when they meet in the kitchen, too dispirited even to make coffee or prepare breakfast. They know that they will not have the energy to fight Alice. When she hasn't appeared by mid-morning they wonder if they should rouse her.

'At least bad dreams don't trouble her,' says Livy bitterly.

'I'll go and wake her,' says Em. 'Let's get it over and done with.'

She goes out – but presently she is back. Her breath comes fast and her face is white.

'Oh, my God,' she says to a startled Livy, 'Alice is dead. She's *dead*. She's lying half out of bed and she's been sick. She looks horrible. Oh, *God*!'

Livy takes the stairs two at a time, Emmy panting behind

her. At the door they pause. Alice is stretched across the rumpled bed, her eyes are open, her face twisted in a horrible rictus grin. Vomit is on the sheet and fragments of food are scattered about. The girls go closer, fascinated and horrified by the sight.

'Has she had a fit?' asks Emmy fearfully. 'She looks awful.'

'What was she eating?' wonders Liv, looking at the fragments of food. 'Some kind of fruit pie?' For some reason she is filled with a terrible foreboding; something nags at the back of her mind and she desperately tries to marshal her wits.

'Should we call the doctor?' asks Emmy anxiously.

'Wait,' says Liv slowly. Carefully avoiding Alice, she picks up a pie which lies intact further down the bed. Without speaking she shows it to Emmy who frowns at it.

'That's one of mine,' she says, puzzled. 'I took them out of the freezer last night ready for today. She must have gone down in the night and pinched them. How like Roop! Perhaps they weren't unfrozen properly . . .'

'Em,' says Liv, holding out the pie. 'Look.'

Frightened by the note in her voice, Emmy peers closer. The sugar has fallen from the pie's crust and there, marked clearly, is a cross.

Emmy shakes her head. 'I don't understand,' she mutters. 'It's one of mine, I'm sure of it, but I don't put crosses on the top like that . . . Aagh!' She puts both hands to her mouth as she remembers. 'Oh, Christ! . . . It can't be,' she shouts at Livy's white face. 'It *can't* be. You threw them away. You said so.'

'*I* said so?' Liv shakes her head. 'I didn't touch them. They were already in the bin.'

'Wait,' says Em. 'Wait.'

They stare at each other whilst Alice stiffens stealthily between them.

'I put the plate on the larder shelf,' says Liv, remembering. 'And when I came back after lunch it was gone but there was a bag in the rubbish. It had little pastry pies in it. I *saw* them.'

'Oh hell.' Emmy sounds as if she might burst into tears. 'I was so groggy that day. Wait. Let me think . . .'

'Not here,' says Liv suddenly. 'The stench is awful. Let's go downstairs for a minute.'

They shut the door behind them and hurry downstairs, still carrying the pie. Liv switches on the kettle whilst Emmy prepares the mugs for black coffee.

'Now,' says Liv as they sit opposite, clutching their mugs. 'Let's go through it very carefully.'

'I picked the berries,' says Em, her eyes closed, 'and came back to the kitchen and cut them into tiny pieces and pushed little bits in with the mincemeat. I had some pastry in the fridge. And . . . and I cooked them.'

'So where,' asks Liv, when Em appears to have finished her recital, 'did the others come from?'

'The others?'

'There were six others,' says Liv carefully and distinctly. 'That's why you marked the poisonous ones with a cross. So as not to get them mixed up.'

'That's right!' cries Em. 'It's coming back now. I found the others in the freezer, left over from Christmas and I took them out with some other things that I thought were too old to use. Some meat pies, that's it! I hadn't labelled them but I knew they were well past eating. I chucked them in the rubbish . . . Oh, no . . .'

They stare at each other.

'So,' says Liv at last. 'The meat pies are in the rubbish. Where did the poisonous ones go?'

Emmy closes her eyes again. 'When Roop arrived,' she says in a monotone, 'I decided not to let him have any lunch. I shoved things into the fridge and there were three mince pies left on the table. I put them in a bag and put them in the freezer.'

'No.' Livy shakes her head. '*I* put the three pies in the freezer.'

'I remember doing it,' protests Emmy. 'I remember scooping them off the plate and grabbing a bag. I *remember* it.'

They sit in silence, staring at the pie with the cross on its pastry cover.

'Hang on,' says Liv. She goes into the larder and fiddles about. Presently she returns with a bag. Inside are three mince pies. She shows them to Em who stares at them, puzzled.

'I simply don't understand,' she says helplessly. 'Two bags with three pies in each. Why? There were six poisonous ones. Where are the other three?'

Liv sits down thoughtfully. 'OK,' she says. 'Let's go back a bit. You put the three good pies in the freezer, straight from the table. The other six are still on the larder shelf where I put them. What did you do then?'

'I came out of the larder,' says Em, eyes shut again, so as to recreate the scene, 'from putting the pies in the freezer and Roop was in the kitchen. I said something like, "Lunch is over. Tough luck." I remember that I was feeling ill, really awful. And I went straight upstairs to bed. I didn't wait to see them off.'

'And I was fussing about with Rosie,' remembers Liv slowly, 'while Roop was all on his own in the kitchen . . . Or in the larder.'

Their eyes meet. Emmy swallows.

'Oh, God,' she whispers. 'You mean that *Roop* ate them?'

'He would have gone into the larder,' says Liv, 'and poked about like he always did. I'd pushed them back on the shelf and half covered them but I bet he saw them. He brought the plate into the kitchen . . . but why?'

'I can guess why,' says Emmy suddenly. 'He wanted to show me that he'd beaten me. That he'd found something which he thought I'd hidden from him. It was a kind of "Yah boo sucks!" How like Roop. He ate three pies, then, and when you saw the other three, you put them in the freezer thinking they were the ones we'd had at lunch.' She looks pleased at having arrived at this deduction; at solving the mystery.

Livy stares at Em. She is waiting for her to arrive at the next conclusion. She watches the satisfaction fade from Em's face and horror take its place.

'Oh, Christ!' gasps Emmy. 'So that's why Roop had the accident. The poison started to work and he crashed the car. Oh, God! I killed them. I killed Rosie and Roop.'

'And *I* killed Alice,' says Liv grimly. '*I* put the pies back in the freezer.'

There is another silence.

'What shall we do?' whispers Emmy.

'We'll have a drink,' answers Liv, 'while we're deciding.'

# 23

By the time they have had several drinks apiece, they are feeling calmer. The horror fades a little.

'We didn't *really* kill them,' announces Livy suddenly.

'Didn't we?' asks Em hopefully, ready to be convinced.

'No,' says Liv, reaching for the bottle. 'Greed killed them. Greed killed all three of them, one way or another.'

'Oh,' says Emmy. She hiccups. 'Good. That's all right then.' Something, however, is nagging at her, refusing to let her be comforted. 'So what shall we do about Alice?'

Liv sits brooding. 'With Alice dead,' she says, 'there's no one left to bother us. The trouble is . . .'

She hesitates so long that Em becomes anxious again and reaches, in her turn, for the bottle.

'What?' she asks. 'What *is* the trouble?'

Liv screws her eyes up, the better to think. 'We don't want people getting suspicious,' she points out. 'They might think we killed her because she was going to throw us out. See?'

Em nods. Yes, she sees. All is clear so far.

'I wonder if anyone knows she's here?' muses Liv. 'She turned up very mysteriously, didn't she? Wouldn't say how she got here, would she?'

Emmy is nodding sagely, uncertain as to where this catechism is leading.

'So,' says Liv, 'supposing she never arrived at all? Supposing we haven't seen her?'

Emmy, who is continuing to nod with her eyes shut, stops abruptly. Her eyes fly open.

'But we *have* seen her,' she says, frowning. 'She's upstairs. Dead.'

Liv sighs heavily. '*You* know that,' she says, leaning across the table. '*I* know that. But does anyone else know it?'

Em tries to concentrate. She understands that Liv is saying something momentous but she can't quite make out what it is.

'I don't know,' she mumbles. 'Why?'

Liv sighs. 'I bet no one knows where she is,' she says. 'She was always sly and cunning. I think she slipped down here to see what was going on and no one has a clue what she's up to. We could deny ever having seen her . . . No one could prove she was ever here.'

Emmy sighs frustratedly. 'But what shall we *do* with her?' she asks.

Liv thinks for a bit. She is determined that nothing now must happen that might put their home at risk; the redecoration, the work in the garden, the new summerhouse . . . Liv straightens up and her eyes begin to glow.

'Emmy,' she whispers. 'I've had a truly brilliant idea.'

'Thank God,' breathes Emmy with relief. 'So what are we going to do?'

Livy beams upon Em. She begins to chuckle. 'You'll never guess,' she warns her.

'No,' says Em. 'I don't suppose I shall. What is it?'

'It's so clever,' cries Liv, roaring with laughter. 'You'll never guess in a million years.'

'Go on, then,' says Emmy, as if they are playing a parlour game. 'I give up. What is it?'

'We're going to put Alice down the well,' says Livy, triumphantly. 'So what do you think of that?'

'Down the *well?*'

'Yes,' says Liv. 'Listen. Joe made that lovely wooden cover, remember? It fits flush with the paving. He calls it a . . . former. Something like that. Now, we will lift the former and put Alice down the well and put the lid on her. Tomorrow, Joe is coming to lay the concrete and . . . there we are. Goodbye, Alice.'

'Goodbye, Alice,' repeats Emmy thoughtfully.

'Nobody but you and I will know,' whispers Liv. 'And we shall never breathe a word to a living soul.'

Emmy shakes her head obediently. 'Never,' she repeats.

Liv looks at her. There is much to be done and there must be no mistakes. She removes the bottle from Em's reach and stands up.

'We need a very large bag,' she says, 'or a sack. And we shall need the wheelbarrow. Come on, Em. Get a grip! We've got work to do.'

When it is dark, Alice comes downstairs. She bumps down in an old sack which Emmy and Liv carry between them.

'Careful,' whispers Liv as Emmy stumbles and Alice starts crashing down on top of her. She braces herself against the weight. 'Gently does it.'

Panting heavily, the sack rough in her sweating palms, Emmy lowers Alice step by step. The bedroom is clean as a whistle, sheets washed, all signs of occupation removed. Alice's few belongings are in the bag with her. The girls have puzzled over the syringe and noticed the tiny puncture marks and bruises on Alice's skin but now there is nothing to see except the bulgy sack, going downstairs one step at a time.

They carry her through the dark hall – 'No lights,' warns Liv, 'someone might see in' – along the shadowy corridor and out of the back door. By the step waits the wheelbarrow. Alice fits quite well into its deep curves but Emmy holds tight to the sack as Liv wheels the barrow along the path and across to the yard. The heavy cover has been raised in readiness and, when they reach the dark corner, they drag Alice out and together they push her down into the spaces of the well. They wait for the splash to echo up before they lift the heavy wooden former back in place. It has been specially strengthened in readiness for the concrete and it drops back with a satisfactory clunk.

Emmy and Liv stand for a moment in the pitchy silence. It is overcast but dry and there is no sound but the mournful cry of an owl in the woods. Emmy shivers suddenly and Liv seizes the handles of the empty wheelbarrow. They go back together, checking the barrow carefully, sweeping round it with their hands, before wheeling it into the shed. Back inside, they stand together in the kitchen, waiting, listening.

'We're safe,' breathes Livy in Em's ear.

Emmy squeezes Liv's arm. 'Safe,' she mutters.

The days pass. Summer draws on and the new summer-house is erected on its concrete base. Joe picks up a barbecue second-hand and initiates Livy and Em into the joys of *al fresco* food. Most evenings they can be found barbecuing beside the summerhouse with a box of supermarket wine on the rustic table close at hand. Em, wrapped in a huge apron, hums gaily as she turns the sausages; 'Over my shoulder goes *one* care,' whilst Liv, topping up their glasses, gives an imitation of Jessie Matthews tap-dancing her cares away. When they have practised enough to their own satisfaction they give a little barbecue party which is an enormous success. The wine flows like water and there are strawberries, grown in the kitchen garden, served with cream for pudding.

Their stock in the village soars even higher and Joe is very proud of 'my old girls', as he calls them. Livy and Em become the doyennes of the car boot sales but, despite this useful income, they wonder if they can manage, even at their present level of existence, for more than another five or six years.

'We'll have to start selling the really valuable things,' says Em sadly.

'Let's wait and see,' says Liv. 'We can get by for a bit longer yet.'

When Jackie comes in one morning she is bursting with happiness.

'I'm pregnant,' she tells them. 'I never thought I would be. I reckon it's coming back here and life slowing down and being calmer and everything. Joe's got plenty of work on and we've got no mortgage and we've been so happy this summer . . .' and running out of words and breath alike, she lays her head down on the kitchen table and weeps.

Emmy and Liv bustle about, insisting that they must drink to this wonderful news, getting in the other's way, laughing and joking, and, when Joe puts a bashful head inside the door, they both cheer him loudly.

Later, they go up to the attic and find the Silver Cross pram so that the baby can bask on the terrace whilst Jackie is working in the house.

'It'll be nice,' says Emmy cautiously, watching Livy, 'to have a baby around.'

'It will,' agrees Liv, all her griefs forgotten. 'Listen, Em. Supposing we leave everything to Jackie and Joe? Whichever one of us goes last, I mean. What do you think?'

'I think it's a brilliant idea,' says Em. 'This house needs a family going on in it, not sold up to be a nursing home. Or flats.'

There is a tiny remembering silence.

'We won't tell them, though,' says Liv. 'Just in case.

We don't want to unsettle them. Not while the deadly nightshade still grows in the woods.'

They begin to laugh, watching each other slyly, laughing until the tears come.

'What's the joke,' asks Joe, appearing in the doorway.

'Never you mind,' retorts Liv, swallowing down her chuckles. 'Come and lend a hand with this pram.'

The kitchen garden flourishes; delicious fresh vegetables are served up at every meal and the freezer is filled against the cold winter days. Freeman – or Hardy – or Willis – dies and, one day, Liv arrives home from shopping with two Persian kittens.

'Saw the advertisement in the paper a couple of weeks ago,' she tells the delighted Em. 'Must keep up the tradition.'

'They are *so* pretty,' cries Em, 'but whatever shall we call them?'

'Easy,' grins Livy. 'It came to me in a flash. We'll call them Russell and Bromley.'

The sun pours down from a cloudless sky and sometimes Emmy is able to believe that the Alice affair was a kind of nightmare. This is especially possible when she has been making frequent use of the flask. The whole thing seems hazy and unreal. Surely it couldn't have been possible?

'Sometimes,' she says to Livy, 'sometimes I have the most peculiar dream.'

'Oh yes?' Livy waits, sitting quite still.

'Yes.' Em peeps at her slyly, rather like Mo used to when she knew she was being naughty but hoping to get away with it. 'It's always the same. I dream that we poison Alice and put her down the well.'

Livy begins to laugh. She laughs and laughs until Emmy

laughs with her. The tears stream down their faces and they rock to and fro in their seats.

'Down the well,' moans Liv, wiping her eyes. 'Down the *well*?'

'I know,' agrees Emmy. 'Isn't it crazy?'

They look at one another, perfect understanding between them.

'Crazy.' Liv shakes her head. 'Comes of eating cheese for supper. I've told you before. Down the well. Honestly! We haven't *got* a well.'

They stare at one another.

'No,' says Emmy after a moment. 'No, of course we haven't.'

The private detective employed by Roop's lawyer arrives to make enquiries about Alice; unless she is found the estate cannot be distributed. The sisters keep their eyes carefully away from the newly-creosoted walls and the basket chairs set out on the verandah of the new summerhouse and take him into the kitchen. Whilst they make coffee and hunt for a stray biscuit, Livy and Em discourse quietly together, and with a gentle regret, on the vagaries of their niece: the detective makes unobtrusive notes and asks the odd question or two. Emmy and Liv murmur about Alice's proclivity for taking off without warning to foreign fields; her back-packing trips with undesirable companions and the risks involved with hitchhiking. The word 'drugs' is whispered with a kind of anxious horror. They confirm that they receive no letters or telephone calls from Alice and ask each other – somewhat fruitlessly – how long it has been since they saw her. They agree that she has never had much time for her family and speak of the distress and unhappiness she has brought her parents, at which point Emmy becomes visibly emotional and Liv hastens to comfort her.

The detective explains that if Alice cannot be traced then, seven years after their deaths, Roop's and Rosie's estate will be divided between their next of kin. He finishes his coffee, promises to pass on any news and climbs into his car; the two women wave him off, watching until the car reaches the bottom of the drive and passes out through the gateway. They stand together for a moment in silence. The dull roar of the motorway is heard more clearly on such a breathlessly hot morning and the smell of the creosote mingles with the scent of the honeysuckle which cascades over the garage roof. Without speaking they turn their steps towards the summerhouse. They seat themselves in the chairs on the verandah, looking beyond the sloping lawn and the topmost branches of the trees that grow in the valley below; away to the distant hills.

'Seven years,' muses Emmy thoughtfully.

'Six now,' points out Liv. 'Give or take.'

Emmy sighs contentedly and turns her face to the sun. 'It's lovely here,' she says.

'It's funny,' says Liv, after a moment, 'if you close your eyes the noise of the motorway sounds exactly like the sea.'